A. P. Laughlin

**Fritz in America**

A. P. Laughlin

**Fritz in America**

ISBN/EAN: 9783337343446

Printed in Europe, USA, Canada, Australia, Japan

Cover: Foto ©Andreas Hilbeck / pixelio.de

More available books at **www.hansebooks.com**

# A DRAMA.

## In Three Acts and Three Scenes.

### By A. P. LAUGHLIN.

With Stage Directions, Characters, Costumes, Etc.

———

VALLEY PRINT, DECATUR, ALA.

# CHARACTERS.

FRITZ German American, vender of fruits and flowers.
COL. ROSTAND BRANCH—Ex-Confederate officer.
TOM GALBRAITH—Heir to Galbraith Hall; nephew to Col. Branch.
MAJ. PHILIP McGREGOR Major in Federal army.
HERR GEOPPER— German Gentleman.
FLYBURGER—Dude- attendant to Herr Geopper.
FIRST OFFICER.
SECOND OFFICER.
PAUL Colored servant to Branch.
GABRIAL—Colored Servant.
JONES—Squire.
TOMMY—Little son of Tom Galbraith and Cleo.
CLEOPATRA—Supposed Octoroon, in love with Col. Branch; subsequently wife of Tom Galbraith.
ALLIE—Daughter of Col. Branch, wife of Maj. McGregor.
HARRIET SIMMONS—Rich old maid.
TRACY—Daughter of McGregor and Allie, stolen in infancy by Branch and reared by Fritz and Cleo, finally Fritz's wife.
KATRINE—German servant.
MARY LUCY—Colored servant.

# COSTUMES.

FRITZ—Act. I.—Short coat of Federal private soldier, with remainder of citizens clothes, knee pants. Act II. Same as Act I, without soldier coat. Act III. At first similar to act II. As Herr Geopper, elegant gentleman's attire of present day; as Katrine, mother hubbard of coarse material. Finally black dress suit with knee pants and black stockings.

BRANCH.—Act I. Colonel's Suit of Confederate grey. Act II. Citizen's suit with black cape. Act III. Black suit with high-topped boots, with spurs.

GALBRAITH.—Citizen's attire, to suit the times.

McGREGOR.—Suit of Federal Major.

FLYBURGER.—Rank dude attire.

OFFICERS.—Blue, with brass buttons.

JONES, PAUL, GABRIEL.— Plain clothing.

TOMMY.—Child's suit of present day.

CLEO.—Act I. Red dress with short, full skirt, black bodice and shoulderstraps. Act II. Similar to Act I. Act III. Elegant house dress of present day.

ALLIE.—Act I. Blue silk with lace overdress. Act II. Ragged garments of coarse material. Act III. Ragged outer dress, and traveling dress of to-day.

HARRIET SIMMONS.—Act I. Full, large-figured silk, festooned, over balmoral skirt over large hoops. White waist, short cut-away sack with long, flowing sleeves over lace undersleeves, high scoop bonnet. Act II. Evening dress.

TRACY.—Act. I. Infant's dress. Act II. Child's dress with bare arms and neck. Act III. As a miss of to-day.

MARY LUCY.—Plain girl's dress.

# FRITZ IN AMERICA.

## ACT I.

SCENE—Lawn—Large hollow tree in center. Enters Cleopatra, an Octoroon.

*C.* Not here? Not here? Surely it can't be much before the time. I watched the clock and gave myself scarce fifteen minutes time to get here. But (laughs) the wings of my most ardent love did bear me on most swiftly. Why, really 1 am quite out of breath. Oh, Rostand Branch, how I do love you! love you! love you! Ah me! how that lacks of expressing what I feel for my most grand of sweet-hearts.

> There's magic in the slightest glance
> That I may gain from thee,
> I'm bound in an ecstatic trance
> If you but smile on me.

Ah me! how vain the warning of my dear dead mother not to love a white man. "Cleo," said she. "Cleo let me wa'n you, de day you lows yo'self to lub a white man, dat day you signs and seals yo' doom. How does I know?" says she. "Lor now honey, how I *does* know. Good Masta what I done suffered at de hands ob yo' dead daddy. Oh, no chile, don't ask me how I knows; don't ask me nuffin. Didn't he come to me wid his smiles and his sweetful talk and be so sof wid me, and tell me how he lub me and how purty I war, and how he'd be so truc to me and dis and dat, and den bress de Lor honey 'fo' you could walk didn't he come to me drunk and 'bukeme and den worse dan all didn't he go and marry Miss Maria and den tell me to go marry some nigga whats my equals.Lor chile," says she, " lc' me tell you, 'fo' God don't you be 'preciatin' ob dese white men. You lub some nice colo'd man whats not ashamed to marry wid ye." But angel mother, sweet as you were ignorant, how could I help but love my Rostand. Love him yes and he loves me, and he shall marry me. But deary me, Cleo, how you rare? (Looks about.) Not coming yet? I'll chide my tardy lover. I can't have missed the time he said, but I'll read again his note and see. (Reads)—

"MY PRECIOUS LITTLE SWEET-HEART—(Say he don't love me)—Please be sure to meet me at the old hollow tree in the morning at six o'clock, —promptly at six. Come alone, of course. I have something of importance to say to you, a proposition to make, if you please—(hear that)—that will try your love for me. It is useless for me to say: do not disappoint me.

Yours as ever and forever,<br>ROSTAND BRANCH."

Disappoint you Rostand, my beloved, never, never. But I fear unless he comes I'll be the disappointed party. (Looks about). Ah! he comes. Gracious me! sit still my heart. (Seems embarrassed.) What shall I do? What shall I say? Shall I be de-demonstrative and rush into his arms? or shall I be dignified and say: My lord is a laggard in love to-night. Most likely I shall do neither. (Looks again.) Why, he's carrying something—a basket—what can it be? It must be something very particular or he'd have it carried. Dear me, I'm so impatient. Oh, I think I'll hide in this hollow tree and fool him. (Hides in the tree.)

(Branch enters and looks around.)

B. Why, my angel don't seem to fly to-day.

C. (Jumping out.) Don't she, 'ha, ha, ha. (Laughs heartily.)

B. (Kissing her.) Whist—whist. Don't laugh so boisterously, Honey, you'll wake the baby.

C. Ha, ha; what have you got in that basket. (Tries to see.)

B. No, no, darling, you shall know by and by; there's something weighty there.

C. (Taking basket.) Let me see—not so very. Pray what is it?

B. (Takes basket and puts it on the ground.) What is it?

Something of great moment. I mean, Cleo, something pertaining to my business here with you. Something I trust you will not shrink from.

*C.* What, the proposition? No, indeed. Shrink from a proposition of a gentleman? Ha, ha; that's not what ladies are said to do. But really a proposition that takes a basket to contain it seems quite ominous. But how have you been, my love, since last we met? it seems so long.

*B.* Well, I thank you, physically. But Cleo, dear, I have been most sick at heart, I assure you. I assure you, my dear, most sick at heart.

*C.* Oh, my own dear what can it be, what can it be? Please let me know, do tell me quick. I am sure no one will sympathise with you as your own Cleo. Come, my love, what can so trouble your most precious heart?

*B.* (Taking her hands and placing her arms about his neck and taking her face in his hands.) Cleo, it is something dreadful and you, and you alone can help me. You can if you will, and if you will I'll promise anything.

*C.* Gracious, me! What can it be? As old Miss used to say, you've quite unstrung my nerves; but really Colonel aren't you going to propose? (Laughs.)

*B.* Come, Cleo, do be serious a little while. Please have done with nonsense, I have. Pray would you have me propose to you every time we meet?

*C.* I like to have you tell me how you love me. But tell me, what are your troubles, and what can I do to alleviate them?

*B.* You remember, Cleo, more than a year ago when the Yankees were here, you know they camped in my lawn—the General had his headquarters in my house.

*C.* Yes, I remember distinctly — what handsome men they were.

*B.* Hush, please, Cleo. Well, among the General's staff was a young officer by the name of McGregor—Philip McGreger.

*C.* Yes; handsome, wasn't he?

*B.* Oh, yes; very good looking—but—

*C.* And Miss Allie fell in love with him! Oh, how delightful! how romantic!

*B.* Do be quiet, Cleo.

*C.* Well, dear me, it's just like a novel—a love affair between a Southern girl and a Yankee soldier; ha, ha.

*B.* This is nothing to be amused at, Cleo. It's much too serious an affair. But you have anticipated rightly. Poor, dear Allie was so young. That Yankee rascal in my absence, with his wily arts, won the affections of my daughter, my *daughter;* think Cleo. When I returned and learned of this dreadful affair, I could have killed the dog. But that is nothing to what followed. I forbade my daughter's seeing him again. In a short time the troops were moved from here, and I though , of course, now that this inconvenient Yankee was out of her sight, Allie would soon forget him. But alas! alas! under the pretense of visiting her aunt she went to Baltimore, and there according to pre-arrangements, met this Yankee McGregor again, and would you believe it Cleo, she married him. Yes, she married him.

*C.* She did! oh dear me how delightfully romantic. Do pray go on. Colonel, what did they do next?

*B.* If you'll give me the opportunity I'll tell you. Soon after she married she wrote to me that as the war had progressed to such an extent that traveling was attended with a good deal of danger, she would remain and attend school. Thinking her safe with her aunt I readily concurred with her and permitted her to remain, especially as I was away from home a great deal, and she would thus be left so much alone here.

*C.* And all this time while everybody has been thinking her away at school she has been playing the romantic girl and living in all the bliss of a clandestined marriage. Dear me, and is that the dreadful thing that troubles you? I am sure that is nothing to worry about.

*B.* What Cleo! Nothing! nothing! I, a Southern gentleman and my daughter runs off and marries a Yankee soldier, and I not worry!

*C.* Yes; but then he was so handsome she couldn't help but love him, and she was so spunky and independent; I wouldn't have thought it of little Allie. Why, Colonel, you ought to be proud of her.

*B.* Are you mad, Cleo! are you mad! that you talk to me thus indifferently about such a calamity?

*C.* Oh, dear me, Colonel. The thing is just splendid. Just like a lovely story. But where are they now?

*B.* Listen: Allie's marriage is a secret here and it must remain such, and what I ask of you is to help me keep it so.

*C.* Surely I will, but how better than to say nothing about it. As mammy used to say, " The good book says a wise head totes a still tongue."

*B.* Quite true, Cleo. But there is sometimes stronger evidence than that given by the word of mouth. And there is stronger proof of this unfortunate marriage than that which might be ignored as hearsay. The thing is much worse than you imagine :

After the surrender, Allie not coming home, I went after her, and horror of horrors, I found her sick in a Catholic hospital with a right young baby, perfectly penniless, and her husband nowhere to be found. While she was there I did everything I could to induce her to leave the child in an orphan asylum, as it was my intention from the first to suppress the matter. But she actually came near dying. And the physicians assured me that it would either cause her death or the loss of her mind to take the child away. On the way home we stopped in the mountains where we were not acquainted. The mountain air strengthened Allie, but her baby grew more delicate, and finally, by stratagem I convinced her the child died, and to-day she thinks it buried at Blue Mountain Home. But the baby did not die, and being unable to conceal it there, I secured the service of a negro to bring it on, he traveling on the same train with us. On arriving here, I thought first, of course of you, and Cleo, darling, there it is in that basket. I want you to help me make away with it.

   *C.* In that basket! the baby? You frighten me. How stupid of me not to have thought it at first. But oh, Colonel Branch, I can't, I can't; dear me, think how unjust to poor Miss Allie. Poor, poor Miss Allie—and oh how wicked! I can't, I can't.

   *B.* Don't be foolish, Cleo. Although I'd a great deal rather, its not necessary to kill it.

   *C.* (Screams.) Don't speak to me of such a thing! I won't hear it! *I a murderess!* Oh dear, (cries) oh dear. How dare you ask me to do such a thing. Who am I, to be so misused!

   *B.* Who indeed! no one to dare to question me as to my actions or motives I can assure you. By George, indeed, and who am I to be thus addressed by a—well, if it weren't that I do love you, Cleo, I'd take a stick and ware you out. That I would, that I would you little fool.

   *C.* (Still crying.) But indeed I cannot, I cannot, I cannot.

   *B.* Cleo, this seeming conscientiousness of yours quite surprises me. It's scarcely worth your while to seem so just. If I remember rightly Allie's mother dealt not so kindly with you. Although, ha, ha, I am compelled to own she did not kill you.

   *C.* No, through your mean instigation she sold from me my mother and made life without her, than death ten thousand times more wretched.

   *B.* Well, Cleo, if Allie's mother treated you so badly, there's her grand-child and Allie's her daughter, why not be revenged on them.

   *C.* No, Colonel Branch, I am still too young to know anything of revenge. At least to reveng the guilty on the innocent.

*B.* Well, then Cleo, if you wont do it because you hate Allie's mother do it because you love her father.

*C.* I won't, I won't, I won't. (Stamps her foot.) How dare you insist in repeating that obnoxious proposition to me.

*B.* Easy enough, my darling. Listen, that baby is between you and me; must it always be so and you and I remain apart, or will you remove it from between us that we may live together?

*C.* Col. Rostand Branch, are you heartless, and must I needs in hell abide that I may live with you! Ah yes, I see, I know, for devil, indeed, art thou.

*B.* You think you're mighty smart; but its just as I tell you, unless you make off with that child I'll know no more of you.

*C.* Ah, well, said my mammy, Cleo the day you learn yourself to love a white man that day you sign and seal your doom. Rostand Branch, do you mean this?

*B.* Mean it, of course I mean it, and more, not only will I not know you but no one else will want to know you.

*C.* I might have known, I might have known. God forgive me, I'll lend myself to the devil. Well, and if I do what then?

*B.* Said I not I'd promise you anything?

*C.* Yes, but you have always promised without this dreadful thing. Am I still to expect nothing but promises?

*B.* Cleo, I'll do anything, anything you ask if you'll but save me from this disgrace.

*C.* Suppose I ask what may seem a greater disgrace?

*B.* There can be none—nothing that I would so object to. For Cleo you know it has always been intended since the death of Judge Galbraith that Tom and Allie should marry, and if I can sink this affair with the yankee officer it may yet not be too late. Let's hear it Cleo, and it shall be granted, (she hesitates) out with it gal—'even to the half of my kingdom.'

*C.* Make no rash promises. Is it worse for a southern lady to marry a yankee than for a southern gentleman to marry a colored woman?

*B.* What can you mean, Cleo?

*C.* I mean just this: If I do this dreadful thing will you marry me?

*B.* You can't mean it!

*C.* But I do. I do mean it. I'll have no middle ground. The only way you made me entertain a thought of this wicked thing was to threaten to leave me entirely. Now the only way you can make me consent to commit it is to consent to be with me entirely.

*B.* But, Cleo, why can't we live on in the old way. You always seemed to be happy enough and contented.

C.   But I am tired of the old way.   Why not let Allie and McGregor live on in the way they expected to.   They were doubtless happy and contented.   Come, we may be interrupted.   Its right now or never.   What do you say?

B.   But Cleo you know I love you more than any other woman, what more can you ask?

C.   You know what more I ask.   Shall it be yankee son or darkey wife?   (Fritz is heard in the distance warbling and crying apples for sale)   There is Fritz coming, what do you say?   He'll soon be here and I'll be off and you'll be left with the baby to hold.

B.   Great heavens, Cleo! how can you exact so much! (Fritz is heard nearer.)

C.   What do you say?

B.   I promise you faithfully Cleo, I'll never marry any one else.

C.   I am done with promises.   Sware it!

B.   (Holding up his right hand) By all the Gods of heaven, Cleo, I sware I'll never marry any one but you.

C.   That is still not sufficient.   *Sware that you will marry me.*

B.   Cleo, Cleo, you're unjust.   (Fritz again nearer.)

C.   Be it so, there's your baby.   (Starts to go and Fritz is heard again.)

B.   Cleo, have mercy!

C.   Sware that you will marry me.

B.   I sware!

C.   You sware what?

B.   I sware I'll marry you.

C.   (Takes bible from her bosom.)   That is not sufficient, here kiss this Bible and say, Cleopatra, by all the Gods of heaven I sware I'll marry you.   So help me God.

B.   (Takes bible and tremblingly obeys.)   Cleopatra by all the Gods of heaven I sware I'll marry you, so help me God.

C.   (Hiding basket in tree) There it's safe until Fritz passes. Why don't the baby cry?

B.   Its drugged, but it may wake by and by.   Be careful about the dutchman.   Good-bye, I must be off.

C.   Good-bye, Col. Branch.   (She follows him off the stage and Fritz enters with apples for sale.)

F.   A-apples! a-apples—fine apples! fine apples!—apples, apples—fine maiden-blush apples.   Vell, I youst dinks dot dutchman could been careful mit his own self.   I tole you vot kind of funny bishness vas dot.   Dot man vash shoore mit ter bible.   By Got in himmel he would marry mit dot gal, Here vas somedings vot I youst put down.   I vitnish dot.   (Cries his apples and effects not to see Cleo as she enters) Been keerful about dot Dutchy, he youst better as been keerful of dot neegar.

C. (Striking him on the back) What nigger?

F. Dot vas you vot vas a neegar!

C. You lie, I'm not a niggar!

F. Vell vot vas you den, of you vasn't a neegar?

C. I am an octaroon.

F. A shpittoon! Vell I don't know of a neegar vas vorser as a shpittoon.

C. I didn't say a spittoon, I said an octaroon.

F. Vell dot vas a neegar dot vas called a coon.

C. I said an octaroon.

F. Vot kind of a mushroom vas dot?

C. Oh you're a fool, Fritz.

F. (Walking up and standing beside her) Vel den you vas de next ding to a fool, (both laugh) But say, Cleo, who vas dot vellew?

C. Who?

F. Dot fellow dot tole you to search dot Dutchman, vot vas me.

C. Oh, he is a very nice gentleman. He did not tell me to search you.

F. Vell, but vot vas his name?

C. Branch.

F. Yhaw, yhaw, dot vas a long branch.

C. (Aside) If I must, I must. The die is cast, but dear, oh, dear, I can't destroy that baby. Oh, I have it, I'll get it off on to Fritz. (Aloud) Say Fritz, come sit down on this log and lets talk. I havn't seen you since we helped those soldiers through that night. Didn't we do that slick?

F. Yah, but one of dem yankee soldiers dun me a yankee trick. He told me vould I sold him by liquor and ven I told him I vould he trunk it up and haunt me back de bottle and say he gib me dot for de viskey, ven I tole him he did not bargain for de bottle, dot it vas mine already, den he said he did not want de bottle; den I tole him he pay me for de liquor ven he say he gib me de bottle for de viskey. I say I not verstant some bishness like dot. It sheems dot vay, but dot vas queer dot I sold mine viskey and don't got nodings, dot I don't vas got already.

C. Oh well, you ought to be glad he had the bust head from drinking it instead of you. Come sit down on this log and lets talk.

F. I don't care, it vas pad viskey anyhow.

C. (Aside) I'll make him serve my purpose, (aloud) Say, Fritz; do you know—did you ever think how friendless I am.

F. (Aside) I guess she vants to marry. (Aloud) Oh now, Cleo

vas frientless?

C. Yes, Fritz, entirely friendless. I am all, all alone.

F. Vere vas I, of I don't been mit you? Vas I been nodings?

C. You did't understand me Fritz. You are sitting here with me now, but you wont be here long and you'll go away and leave me, and I must go home to my cottage alone—all alone—and no one there to keep me company.

F. (Aside) Now I know she vants to marry. (aloud) I'll keep you company Gleo.

C. You don't know what you say, Fritz. When you found your customers leaving you because you kept my company, then you'd see your mistake and leave me.

F. I wouldn't, Gleo, I wouldn't.

C. You called me a negro just now, and perhaps I am, I hardly know what I am. I feel like the bat in the fable, I am neither beast nor bird.

F. You vas youst a vomen, dots vot you vas.

C. Yes, but I am so friendless, I have no one to love. I never had any brothers and sisters. My mother is dead and my father would not own me and—and—oh dear, oh dear, (cries.)

F. (Pittyingly) Oh dot vas too pad, Gleo, don't you do dat now, I love you.

C. (Still crying) No you don't, no one loves me.

F. (Boo, boo, cries) You youst most bust my heart, Gleo. (cries loudly)

C. Fritz did you say you would be my friend?

F. Yes, boo-hoo, ye-ye-yes.

C. A very good devoted friend.

F. (Aside) I vonders if I youst got to shoore I vill marry her too. (aloud) Yes, a very devoted friend.

C. Oh I am so glad—I am so happy.

F. (Chuckles her under the chin) Hootsy, kootsy, pootsy, of you vas happy den I vas happy, den ve vas a douple happy, a great big happy. (laughs)

C. Well then, Fritz, if we are to be devoted friends lets make a contract and sign it with our blood.

F. Ten vould ve been plood kin?

C. I don't know—maybe.

F. Gleo I youst ruther as been friends or shoeethearts.

C. All right, Fritz, any way, (takes pencil and a blank book from her pocket) will you write it or shall I?

F. You, Gleo, my writing don't vas been enough good.

C. All right here goes then. (writes and reads aloud) This-is-to-certify-that-I·Fritz—What is your name anyhow, Fritz?

F. Vot vas my name? You know vot vas my name. It vas youst the same. It vas Fritz.

C. Your real name is Frederick, isn't it?

F. Nine, my real name vas *Fritz*.

C. What is your name then besides Fritz?

F. Tere vas no podish name along te side of my name Fritz.

C. You don't understand, I guess. What name do you have besides Fritz?

F. I vould have you beside me and and dot vould been Cleo beside Fritz.

C. Ha, ha, Well, what vas your father's name?

F. His name vas Fritz.

C. What vas your grand father's name?

F. I guess dot vas Fritz too. They vas all been Fritz' dot I knows.

C. Well [reads] this is to certify that I, Fritz [writes and reads] do hereby agree to be-a-devoted-friend-to—

F. Tere Cleo vot vas your name?

C. Don't you know my name is Cleo.

F. Yah, but vot else next to der side of Cleo.

C. My name in full is Cleopatra.

F. Cleopatra!

C. Yes, don't you know? Cæzar's sweetheart.

F. Vat vas dot you doles me?

C. Cæzar's sweetheart. [F. misunderstands her. Thinking she says seize your sweetheart gets up and jumps around in ɔɪ joy.]

C. What is the matter?

F. Oh I feel so funny. Can you mean it?

C. [Stands] Why certainly I mean. Why not?

F. Tid you say seize yer sweetheart?

C. Yes, Cæzar's sweetheart. [Fritz rushes at her and embraces her. She struggles and frees herself] What do you mean, you impudent fellow; how dare you be so rude!

F. [Crying] Yer dole me ve could been shveethearts and I thought you vas said seize-yer-shveetheart and I vas so glad I youst done it.

C. Well you misunderstood me. Cæzar was a great man and was in love with a queen by the name of Cleopatra. But come sit down again and lets finish our contract. [they sit again]

F. Vell I vill [aside] Vell of I did missunderstood—I don't made her mate and I youst got von good skveeze. [laughs.[

C. Vell as I was reading: This is to certify that I, Fritz, do hereby agree to be a faithful, devoted friend to Cleopatra. Signed Fritz and Cleo.

F. Say, Cleo, vot vas your name dot vasn't Cleopatra?

C. I am like you, truly, Fritz, I don't got some names vot vasn't Cleo. Now that that is settled I have something to tell you —a secret, Fritz, and if you are really a true devoted friend you will help me keep it. You can help me a great deal.

F. Vot was dot secrets?

C. Listen, Fritz, I got a baby. [Fritz faints, then recovers and jumps to his feet, surprise and wrath alike in his countenance.]

F. A paby! a paby!

C. Yes a bady, that's not so terrible.

F. Gif me dot contract. Mine Got! I don't been some devoted friend to some gals vot got some pabies vot don't been married. Dot vould ruin my pishness.

C. Of course the baby isn't married, Fritz, but its mother is.

F. Vash you married? I thought you said you vas alone and vould been my shveetheart.

C. No, I'm not married, of course; I'm not the baby's mother. Listen, its the child of a very good friend of mine who was in Baltimore at the time of its birth. My friend's husband was a Union soldier, but he was lost in some battle or other and in order to keep the whole affair a secret she sent me the baby to take care of. Now listen, Fritz, when the baby comes of age, she will be a great heiress and we will share the money. Don't you see? I have all the papers and everything to prove the child's identity. Now if I keep the baby it might excite suspicion, but if you take it I'll see that you get money to maintain it.

F. Vere ish dot paby?

C. There it is in the hollow tree in that basket. You take it Fritz. [Fritz takes basket from tree and begins to open it, when laughing and talking is heard outside and he suddenly sets basket down.]

C. Oh Fritz!

F. Oh Cleo!

C. There's somebody coming!

F. There's somebody coming!

C. You take the baby, Fritz.

F. Nine you takes te paby, Cleo.

C. You take it, its yours.

F. You dakes him, he's yours.

C. It is not mine, it is yours.

F. Nine. It vas not mine, he vas yours.

C. You said you'd take it.

F. Vell you brought him here. [talking and laughing outside.]

C. Well I'm going to hide, it will be you and the baby for t.

[hides in tree.]

F. Vell, mine Got, I youst hides too, ten it will been te baby for himself. [attempts to get in the tree with Cleo, she pushes him away.]

C. Go away Fritz, there isn't room in here for more than one.

F. Tere ish, tere ish, I von't go vay. [still tries to get in.]

C. Fritz go away. [approaching parties heard outside. Fritz much frightened, hides his head in the tree and trembles with fear] There is not room in here for two I tell you. [she pushes him away, he falls backward, gets up and looks out, frightened.]

F. Mine Got! Vot lots of beapers! Vat vill I done! Oh, oh, oh!

C. [from tree] Take that baby and go off. [Fritz takes up basket and rushes wildly up and down the stage trying to hide.

C. Who is that coming, Fritz?

F. I don't know, I vas so skeered I could not tole of it vas my mother.

C. Look, Fritz, and see. [he looks.]

F. It vas Mishter Tom Galbraith and Mish Allie Branch.

C. Gracious heavens have mercy! [steps from tree] Fritz, for heavens' sake don't let those people see or know what is in that basket or we are all undone. [She steps into tree again and Fritz takes basket and tries to hide it behind tree at one end of stage as Tom and Allie came in at the other. As they advance Fritz goes on around the tree cleaving close to it. Tom and Allie do not perceive him, nor Cleo in the tree.]

TOM. Allie, dear, what does so oppress you! It is in vain, entirely in vain, that I attempted to attract your attention. I talk to you of our childhood days—halcyon days of yore—when I was all and all to you, love, as you were all and all to me. I am still the same, Allie, the change is alone in you. What can it be? What can I have done that you treat me with such marked indifference?

ALLIE. Oh nothing, Tom, nothing.

T. It must be something. It cannot be that you are displeased that I went into the Confederate army.

A. No indeed, Tom, if it were I should also be displeased at papa, who was in the Confederate army too.

T. One would think so, but you expatiate at such length on the immaculateness of the Federal officers, that one would think you had been in sympathy with the Union. Perhaps you have grown romantic and done something unusual and formed an attachment for some yankee soldier. [laughs.]

A. And what if I have.

T. What if you have, ha, ha, how rediculous, Allie. You'd be too proud to marry him if you did.

A. No Tom, you misjudge me, I could not love a man I did not respect, and if I loved and respected a man I'd marry him as soon if he were a union man as if he were a secessionist.

T. Then, perhaps, you loved and married some plebian yankee; ha, ha, and are too proud to own you are deserted, ha, ha. [by this time they have walked to the other end of the stage, and Fritz is seen on the other side of the tree carefully keeping the tree between him and them]

F. Oh tear, I vonters of I vas evestropping; dot was very wicked of Fritz, but he could not help some. I youst hear vat tat vas bout love and yankee.

A. I am not deserted.

T. Then you admit you are married, ha, ha, well I did not know I was courting some other man's wife.

A. If I am now or ever am, the man that's my husband will be too much of a gentleman to taunt a woman because she does not love him.

T. I did not mean to taunt you, Allie, besides you cannot mean you do not love me.

F. Oh mine Got! sit still mine heart. [strikes his breast.]

T. Think of the days before the war when we rode and drove together. You know it was always intended that you and I should marry

A. That was before the war and the war has worked great changes, and why not in me as well as anybody. Why not I be freed as well as Cleo, or any other slave.

T. Really, Allie, you compel me to think you have learned to love some other man.

A. I'll never learn to love any man.

T. No, the man you marry should be one you had loved always, as you have me from childhood.

A. Look here Tom, let me tell you, I don't no more love you than you do me. I don't care to deceive you and you can't deceive me. You know you love Cleo, and I—well I love another man better than I do you.

T. You are certainly candid.

A. Why don't you be a man, and prove Cleo's identity and marry her? She is certainly beautiful and accomplished.

T. Perhaps Cleo, like you, loves some other man.

A. Well, let us be done with trying to make ourselves miserable simply to gratify the whims of fooliish parents.

T. Yes, but you remember the will. What of my disinheritance if you and I don't marry?

A. Of that another time. We can feign love for one another,

if you choose; but now, Tom, good-bye. I want to be alone, and I'll walk the rest of the way home alone. Good-bye.

T. Well, don't say anything of mine and Cleo s affairs to any one. Some day you must tell me of your escapade with this unknown Federalist. Good-bye. [Exit Tom.]

A. Oh, hapless me! What have I done to be thus wrongly dealt with? At seventeen I have had more of sorrow than I had thought to have had at seventy. It seems but yesterday since I gave my heart to Phillip McGregor. At this very spot we promised to be all to one another. Oh, what unkind hand has torn him from me! Ah, Philip! Phillip! where are you to-day? Where, where are you? If thou art slain and cannot come to me in person, then would'st thou not send thy spirit here to comfort me! I am so lonely, oh, so lonely! [Cries.] No, thou wilt not come, then, nor my sweet babe. Oh, baby! baby! sweet image of thy father! [Cries.] All, all is gone that I would'st live for! Husband! Child!

F. Mine Got! I veals sorry for dot 'omens. I youst wish she vould go vay, so as dot Gleo and me could finish up our leetle bishness.

A. [Sees Fritz.] Why, Fritz, you startle me! Are you there? [F., finding himself observed, is rather angry and sits deliberately down beside the basket and lights his pipe.] No, ma'am, I was not tere, I vas youst right here.

A. That was very unkinp of you to be eavesdropping.

F. I didn't drop nodings.

A. I am afraid you heard what I was saying to myself.

F. Vell, if you know your secrets already, vhy den vat for you tole 'em to yourself again for? And of you tole em to yourself vat for you don't tole 'em in a weisper?

A. Did you hear my sad soliloquy?

F. I don't know of I heard him or not. I don't know who Mr. Soliloquy vas.

A. Fritz, tell me, did you hear what I was saying?

F. I youst tish minute coomes here.

A. Well, Fritz, you must not be ungentlemanly, it is not like you. But, say, what have you got in that basket?

F. Sausage meat.

A. What kind of sausage meat, pork or beef?

F. Dot vasn't pork nor beef, dot vas kid.

A. Oh! Oh! Some strange feeling comes over me! [Wails—looks wild.]

F. Vot vas dot? Vat ails you?

A. Oh, what is it? What can it be?

F.  I youst guess you vas right now going to have some fits.

A.  [Insanely.] Something tells me I am near my child, my pretty baby.

F.  Vas dot me?

A.  No, no; oh, no.

F.  Den dot someding tole you a lie, but yost but me dere vas; nopodish dot vas next to you right now but me.  [Aside.]  Mine Got! I vas skeered.  [Allie keeps crying.]

C.  [Peeping out from tree.]  Fritz, for Heaven's sake, what do you mean?  Go 'way with that basket quick.

F.  Vell, I vill go 'vay now, but I come right back so dat I fix up dot leetle paby pishness mit you; of I don't I'm skeered mit dot paby I makes my foot in it.                                      •

A.  Oh, my husband!  My husband!

F.  [Running to her.]  Vell, here I vas, mine vife.

A.  [Not heeding him.]  Oh, my chil l!  My child!

F.  Vell, which of dem I vas?  You calls me tish vay and dot vay, and makes me so muttled I don't know of I vas your husband or your paby.

A.  Go 'way from me and leave me!

F.  Dot do I vill, right away quick.  I guess you vas von leetle bit on to outside of your head, of you knows vat dot vas.

A.  Where is my baby—where is my child?

F.  Say, romans, vat vas it you vas going to have already.  Say, good-bye.

A.  [Following him.]  Where is my child?  Where is my child?

F.  Say, Miss Branch, dot nightmare vat you vas having in de day-time vas a wild horse.  You told me to go, and now I vas going.  [Seems much frightened.]

A.  [Catches him.]  Tell me!  Tell me, base man—where is my child!

F.  Oh, mine Got in himmel!  I shoore I don't know you got some pabies.  Go 'vay!

A.  [Throwing both arms around his neck she shrieks.]  Fritz!  Fritz!  Where's my child!  Where's my child!  [Fritz, frightened terribly, struggles violently, and after much effort gets loose.  Allie faints and falls.  Cleo slips out from tree and meets Fritz as he is about leaving the stage.]

F.  Cleo, confount you and dot paby you dakes him.  Dot vas to biggest troubles I vas in ever in all my days.

C.  No, Fritz, you take it off and wait till I get Allie safely started home, and then come back and we will fix things.

F.  Vas dot her paby?  I youst knows it vas.  Mine Got, I vas dot skeered!

C. No, no! I don't know! But no, no! She acts very strangely.

F. Vell, Cleo, I comes back purty quick, and dot secrets vas a purty little bit a gal paby of I keeps him. [Exit Fritz.]

C. Oh, dear! Oh, dear! This is dreadful! Oh, miserable wretch that I am, how could I give my assistance to this terrible business. She'll haunt me forever. [Goes up to Allie.] Allie, Miss Allie! Why, what's the matter? Allie, Miss Allie!

A. [Arousing.] Oh, oh, where am I, where am I? What's the matter with me? What has happened? Oh, Cleo, is that you?

C. Yes, Miss Allie, what indeed is the matter? You are here by the old hollow tree. How came you here? Did something frighten you?

A. Oh, yes, here by the old hollow tree. Is my baby in that tree? I am sure it is.

C. [Affecting a laugh.] Your baby? Why, Allie, how funny! Ha! ha! Aue you joking?

A. Ha! ha! Yes, what a joke! [Laughs insanely.] What a joke! My baby, ha! ha! My baby! How ridiculous! Did you see Phillip, Cleo, my husband? Where is he?

C. [Aside.] She's actually going insane [Aloud.] What can you mean about your husband and your child?———

A. [Laughing.] Oh, my baby must be hid in that hollow tree. I am sure it was here but a few moments since. [Looks in tree.] No, oh, no! Where is my baby? Where is my child?

C. Come, Alue, dear, lets go home. Shan't I accompany you? Oh, how fortunate! Here comes your father.

A. Oh, ah, yes; ha, ha, (enters B.)

B. Why, what is this? Allie, what are you doing here? Where is Tom?

A. (Embarrassed.) I—I don't know—oh, yes—I have'nt seen him. I'll—I'll go home with you—with you, papa.

B. Come, Allie. (Aside to C.) Does she know anything of the baby?

C. Not that I know of.

B. You come along, I wish to speak to you.

A. Yes, come, Cleo, a little way with us. (As they go out Tom and Uncle Paul, an elderly colored man, enter the opposite end of the stage.)

T. Well, Uncle Paul, have you concluded to accept my proposition?

P. Not zackly.

T. Why not? Col. Branch is no longer your master, and what attention does he give you that you need show such fidelity to him? Tell me the particulars I so much wish for and I'll see that you are taken care of as long as you live, and Uncle Ros. does nothing for you.

P. I am loaf to break my word, as I tole you all de time when we has conversed on dis particular subjec, an I don do it for no wo'ldly reward. I does it to recompence myself for de sin I 'mitted to dat chile and her parents. When Kizzy and me war married she had a infan' young babe, bout a yeah old. It war a white man's chile and de said looked like de Senataw what stayed one fall bout dem times at your pa's to hunt—and specks it war hisen—as it war pow'ful likely and powerful smart—ticklar smart. Dis war while traveling in Europe wid Mars and Miss—arter Kizzy and me war married. Well, Mr. Galbraith, I didn't take to dat chile see as how it war my wife's and warn't mine, and so one day when de bofe fell into de Danube ribber and as I couldn't swim wid em bofe I just towed de ole lady to de show and de infan had to be goddered home wid de angels. Old Mars was ticlar decomstructed bout dat matter, and he cussed and rared, said I drowned de chile for purpose, and said he never forgib me, and right dar sprung up a strangement twixt him and me, though we had been togedder for years. A few weeks arter dat we war some whar in Germany. Mars Rostund and I war riding in de dust of de eb'nen when we passed a 'oman totin' a little black eyed baby. Pears like Mars got mad wid me ime he seed dat chile. Said it minded him of his own little Cleo, and took on't so I says, says I, Mars Rostund, if I stole dat chile back dar and gib it to Kizzy to bring up for you would you forgive me." He did not hesitate to deliberate but a few short minits when he just said "yes". He stopped wid de buggy under a thick shade tree out from de road. I went back to de 'omen and tole her Mars wanted to talk wid her and hold de chile till she went to de buggy, and while Mars war holdin' ob her 'tention, I just slid like a sarpent or snake and took de chile wid me, and what it war wropped up in and go way down de road whar Mars took me up wid de chile arter he sent de gal back whar she expected to fine' me. And when I heard him say as how some day 'twould bring him two thousand dollars, I knowed he done forgib me.

T. And this little baby has grown up into a woman and is none other than Cleo.

P. Dat am de truf as I lib, I done tole now I trus de Lord she may be 'stered back to her native lan. If de Lord forgive me for de dredful han' I played, I'll do all I kin to contrive her back to her parents.

T. What came of the wraps that were around the child, Uncle

Paul?

P. Dare now, I done forgot dat ar 'ticlar evidence, show now. When I give de chile to Mars. Rostand he say, "Paul dis am some rich man's child," and twar so too. The 'omen what hed de chile war just a nu'se. Mars says, "look to dem tings, Paul, such cloths would 'ticlarize de chile and give evidence who it war, and dat would criminate de party wid de chile and 'vict him ob de stelin' of it, so says he "Paul you take dem tings and 'stroy 'em," and I sented to it.

T. But you did not, did you?

P. No, I done got 'em to dis day.

T. Where are they and what all were there, and what will you take for them?

P. Dere war a red velvet blanket wid a yellow lining and gold finery on it, and some gold letters in one corner, and some close de chile had on at de time wid de same letters worked on 'em. But de mos' evidencein' ticlar de child toted on hits pusson war a little gold locket, wid a scriptin on de outside and two somebodies pictures in de inside, one of a beautiful lady, and one of a man dat I suppose war her husband, and I 'lows day war de chile's parents.

T. And you have all these things Uncle Paul?

P. Ise got em safe, and you can hab 'em any day.

T. I can't express my gratitude, believe me you shall not go unrewarded. I will call for the articles this evening, good by, Uncle Paul. [Exit Paul.] Cleo, my own beloved, you shall yet be mine, my own lawful wife. I shall not stop until I have proven your identity. Oh queen of my heart. Oh lonely flower I shall yet transplant you from the wild woods to the gardens of my fore fathers. [In the midst of this effusion, Tom walks off the stage. Presently Col. Branch and Miss Harriett Simmons enter simultaneously at opposite ends of the stage, he bowing low and she courtesying.]

B. Ah my dear Miss Harriett.

H. Why Colonel, are you here? I am sure if I had known it I should not have come. Oh dear no, I mean I should have come if I had known you were here. Oh my heart—dear me—I mean —I—mean—I—

B. You mean dear lady, while you are glad to meet me here, you would not wish to seem forward enough to intercept me here. I understand, believe me my dear lady.

H. Oh yes to be sure, dear me, how kind of you Colonel, and how clever to read my thoughts so well.

B. Yes, allow me [takes her hand and places her arm in his

they promenade] two souls me thinks with but a single thought.

F. [Aside unobserved by them] dot vos how to get each others money.

B. Two hearts that beat as one.

F. They vas courtin' now. Ven they been married, them old peoples it will be two ones that beat as hard.

B. [Taking her hand]. My dear Miss Hariett, it affords me unspeakable pleasure to meet you thus by chance. 'Tis like when one walks in an unfrequented garden, and when by chance one comes suddenly upon a fair white lily, bending as yet unseen its beautiful white blossoms beneath the weight of the sparkling morning dew.

H. Oh dear now Colonel, that is mighty kind of you to say that if you are in earnest.

B. In earnest, to be sure I am, Indeed, why should not I be? It is not every man my age can have the pleasure of saying tender things to a blushing young lady like yourself. Scarcely out of her teens.

H. [Hiding her face, aside] He's one fooled man. [Aloud] Why Colonel, you're not so old. I'm sure you seem right suple-jointed.

B. [Aside] The old fool! Suple-jointed indeed! [Aloud] Yes but I am not so suple of joint as when I was a youthful West Pointer.

H. But why refer to those old days so long, long gone by? What are past months and years but piles on piles of dead and withered leaves.

B. Quite true, on the future we might muse and speak of fond hopes and bright expectations. [Aside.] When I shall be spending her boasted fifty thousand.

A. And what's the future but a garden bear which must bring forth weeds as well as flowers, whose very seeds and germs are yet not grown, much less not known the warmth and moisture of the rich mould that must throw them up to bud and blossom.

B. Ah yes fair creature. Perhaps then 'twould suit you better did I suggest the present?

H. Yes, yes, dear Colonel, why waste words on what has been and will be, while we have what *is*. [Leans fondly on his breast, then stands erect and exclaims]

Ye days apast, how e'er halcyon thy mayest be!
　Oh future days though bright through all eternity!
What art thou! The present's so sweet to me!

[Relapses onto his breast again with her arms around his neck, when Fritz marches in, stepping to the tune he blows loudly on a bugle. B. and H. spring apart, H. screams and most faints, B. looks mad and shakes his fist behind Fritz's back, who blows his bugle, dances and goes off and B. and H. approach each other.]

H.  Oh dear Colonel do you think we were observed?

B.  Perhaps—our glorious present is not proof against inglorious intrusions. [Aside]  By George, the fool, what if that Dutchman saw me and inadvertantly, tell Cleo so.  [Aloud].  Come sit here my precious bird of Paradise and let me whisper low sweet words of love in thy pink pretty ears, so used to such soft breathings of tender though burning passions of hearts so much and oft enamoured by the bewitching charms of thy form and face that do weave such magic spells about the sterner sex, prostrating men at thy dainty feet.

H.  [Almost giving way with emotion.]  Oh my dear sweet Colonel, how eextatic it is to be so sweetly adressed by one so fondly loved.  [They sit closely.]

B. [Embraces her.]  [Aside]  Would to heaven I could but grasp the bosted fifty thousand as tightly. (Aloud.)  Ah my pretty dear do you not find it lonely in your solitary unmarried life?

H.  I do indeed, and I am so much anoyed in attending to my business affairs.

B.  (Aside.)  Ah, an open door, I'll but step in, ..  (Aloud.) To be sure, and what better thing could you do but marry and put this unwieldy burden on stronger shoulders.

H.  True, true, 'tis so I've thought.  (Aside.)  He's warming up to it.

B  You should be careful to select from all your admirers, of all the men who fain would wed the fair Hattie,—(aside.)  She's never had a chance to marry in her life,—(Aloud.)  Some one capable, some man ef experiehce in such matters to handle well your handsome fortune.

H.  Ah yes, of all my admirers—yes how well said.  (Aside..) He's a fooled man, there is not many men distracted about me. (Aloud.)  But who—who more suitable—but—oh really—I blush to be so bold—who more—

B.  (Aside.)  By George, but this most sickens me.  (Aloud, taking her hand.)  Sweet fair young girl, if I might dare to speak it—think it.—  (Drops on his knees.)  If I might be so presuming —(Fritz rushes in, crying aloud.)

F.  Apples—apples.  (H. rushes screaming to the end of the stage.)

B.  (Fiercely.)  How dare you thus intrude!  You scoundrel!

F.  I don't know of it vas intrudin' to valk in to proad taylight along mit a path vot every podish valks in. I vas mistookin. But say, I dinks ven old peoples like you and dot old vomens is cortin' tey youst petter as go in mit der house and pull der plinds down, und leave sparkin' in de lawn to youngsters vot got sense enough to be shly, and vasn't so old and teaf and blint, they could not see some padish till they steps on 'em.

B. Begone you scamp.

F. All right. (To H.) Say you great long shlim weeping willow twig vot vas going to been a Branch, come back here and stop shedin' tears. (Cries) apples,—fine apples. [Exit.]

H. Ah Colonel, what were you saying? You were about to ask me—

B. [Aside.] If I must, I must. [Aloud.] 'Tis most presuming of one my age—age.

H. Though the head be gray and bald, and the face be wrinkled and dead, if so the heart be young—young.

B. [Aside.] Bald and gray, wrinkled and dead! Indeed, by George. [Aloud.] The heart be young, yes, if so the heart be young.

H. 'Tis all I ask, if so the heart be young. Pray have no misgivings Colonel. Let not the timidity of your manly heart defraud you of the untold bliss that but awaits your grasping to be thine forever.

B. Ahem. [Aside.] It's scarcely worth my while to beg for what is thrust upon me—but I must be gallant. [Kneels.] Adored maiden, idol of my heart, wouldst thou—[Enters Fritz.]

F. [Aside.] He vas youst doin' tem dewotimal evercises some more. [Aloud.] You vas saying your prayers again some more old man, hey! [Branch jumps up and H. screams.]

B. Villain! dog!

F. Vell, you vas a hypocrit vat prayed in public places. Vhy don't you as to good book says, enter in some closets or some secret places ven you say your long prayers?

B. Begone you insolent puppy!

F. [To B.] Say don't you want to buy some apples? [To H.] Here vas some vot youst suit your taste. They vas nice soft mellow apples vot you can eat midt out any teeth.

B. Begone, I tell you!

F. I von't been gone. I youst got as good right on tish camp-meeting ground as any podish. . But I dinks it vas times you sung to doctor's phisology. [Goes off singing "All Hail te Power of Jesus Name let Angles (points to B.) prostrate fall.

H. Oh cruel fate! What were you saying Colonel?

B. Ah yes, [Aside] I am terribly disgusted with this thing,

by George. [Aloud]. But some other time, fair Hattie.

H. No my dear Colonel, now dear me, how unfortunate, but then the course of true love never did run straight. Come sit down again. [They sit.] Now what were you saying Colonel? I'm sure you dare to speak it.

B. Another time I beg—another time. I must have time to frame my words into sentences becoming such occasions. [Aside] By George, me thinks the prize I covet—the fifty thousand is scarcely worth the ordeal of winning.

H. As you please dear Colonel, though I am sure I'd not be over particular. Its the import of what you were saying I am after. [The cries of an infant startle them both.]

B and H. What's that.

B. By George! What can Cleo mean! I must be off. [Standing.] H. reclines lovingly in B.'s arms, he regards her lovingly.

H. Oh stay, stay, my love! [Fritz enters with baby holding it up,] ·Coming events [points to baby] cast their shadows before. [Points to B. and H. who hasten from the stage.]

F. [To baby.] There now little cherub, I dinks ve proke up dot prayer meetin'. They vas mate me tired listening to dose devotional exercises. Ve vast youst go to meet Cleo, of she vas come back from the yard. [Goes off]

(Exit Fritz with baby at one end as Branch enters stealthily at the other.)

B. By the eternals, 'tis the same child! Had I not seen it I'd known it by its voice when it whimpered (steals further in). Would to God I were not such a fiend or that I were doubly so; that I did not want this babe dispatched or that I had will to do it. My God, and am I so soon betrayed! I did not think it of her! Cleo, Cleo! But yet me thinks right often I've seen her in company with this Dutchman, and 'tis but likely he saw me court that old maid Harriet and told Cleo, who deemed I'd broken faith with her, when thus to retalliate she let Frstz know my secret; and am I thus undone? (Goes out and Fritz enters with the basket which he places in hollow tree.)

F. Tere now shtay there, my pretty pet, till I cooms pack. 'Twill joast been but a leetle vhile. I guess you shleeps some all te times veh I been gone. Of Gleo vas come I could not leaves you tene all alone by your leetle self. Goot bye, mine leetle ootsey pootsey; I been back pretty soon quick. (Exit Fritzs—enters Branch, excited.)

B. Me thinks I'm not so weak a fiend as first I'd thought myself to be (pauses.) Where is't! Where is't! But no; but no! It can't be that I've become so base. No; ha, ha! No, not just now become so base, but to myself become some better known, ha, ha. For had I known when, that this baby lived was known to me alone, that I had lack of heart to do this thing, I'd done it. But perhaps 'tis not too late. Did he not bring it here but now? I'll look. [Looks and sees basket in tree.] Ha, the basket,—'tis there. [Peers into basket.] Ha, the covering moves with the little thing's soft breathing. I'll do this thing, but how? I have it, fortune favors me. I've with me now the stuff with which I made the child go to sleep. I've to double the portion but once to double the effect ten thousand times. [Takes bottle from pocket and saturates a handkerchief.] There, I'll assure myself that no one comes, [looks both ways] and nerve myself with a moments cogitation. My daughters fair name, wealth, position and honor, Galbraith Hall for Allie and Mont View for myself, cry out: "This little bud for earth too fair must go to heaven to blossom there." I'll to my task, for he who wills to do a dirty deed and falters is not less the fiend, but more the coward. [Kneels by basket, turning his face away, screaning it with one hand while he thrusts the hand holding the handkerchief into the basket.] I'll turn my face, lest the sight of the baby's face should make me squeemish. It struggles hard but cannot speak. Oh ye devils that put me on to this foul deed, now see me through it. Calmer it grows, and struggles less. 'Tis still—tis dead—dead—and I—

    F. [Rushes in] And you? Vat you doin? Vat you done?

    B. You lie, I have done nothing.

    F. [Examines basket.] Yuo lie, you vas dons sometings, boo—hoo—vat for you killed mine leetle tog! [Draws a stuffed dog from basket and cries.]

    B. A dog? [Aside.] Sold again, by George, I don't know if I should curse or laugh.

    F. Yes my tog? [Fritz cries and pets the dog, then taking it by the tail swings it around and throws it at Branch, knocking him down. Fritz goes off crying.]

    B. By the Gods, Rustand Branch was never so chagrined as now, ha ha, as say the niggers: I got the wrong sow by the ear that time. There is nothing gained that that boy Fritz discovered I'd but killed a dog, for had he known I'd killed the child and dared confrunt me with it, I could as well have said 'twas he, and if he'd pushed me I'd stabbed him to the heart and swore I did it in the child's defense. But, who have we here? How now Cleo, did you see Allie home and safe, and did she become quieter and better reconciled.

    C. No, no, my dear Colonel, and you're hard of heart and

cruel I must say, my love, to practice such unkindness on your daughter.

B.  Do not chide me darling, did I not pay you for your pains.

C.  You did what I required at least.

B.  Then why that sad complaining face?

C.  Because you gave me occasion to require so much of you by requiring so much of me.  Pure love that pulses in pure hearts and makes the face to glow with sweet peacefulness, the soul feels should have naught of requiring.

B.  Then you're dissatisfied my love?  You reconfirm the fears I felt, but banished at sight again of your sweet face, that you had played me false, and let Fritz know my secret.

C.  Fritz?  Oh no, we've a compact though as regards the rearing of the child; to live together at the cottage.  I left the child with him, but now.  [B. draws Cleo's arm in his and they go off as Fritz appears with the child in his arms.]

F. There now, what vas tooks one anothers for better as vorse vas youst better as got acxuainted some.  You vas Tharessa?  Vat! you don't know dot before?  Yah you vas Tharessa, dot vos mine mutter vot vos Tharessa, and dot vos mine sister vot vos Tharessa, and so dot vos my leetle girl vot vos Tharessa.  Yah, yah, and dot vas me dot vas Fritz.  Vat! don't know dot?  Oh yah, dot vas me, Fritz, and I youst-call you Tracy, vot vas Tharessa made quicker, and then ve vos Fritz and Tracy vot vas took one another for better and vorse until death vos not put us apart together, not much.  [The baby cries.]  Oh, vot vos you don't like dot again already, or vos dot some pins a sticken' you?  Nine, oh vos you got some collicks?  [Lays child on his knee face downward and trots it so the baby cries louder.]  Nine; there, there.  [Gets up and shakes baby and walks up and down the stage, baby cries and Fritz sings a German lullaby.]

> Shlof kint line shlof,
>   Ter mutter heat te shof.
> Der fatter heat te brownie coo,
>   Kintline moschdine oint-line tsu,
> Slof kintline slof.

[Baby cries, Fritz sings, shakes baby and walks back and forth as curtain falls.]

---

## ACT II. ·

### (Three years later.)

SCENE.—Interior of Cleo's cottage.  Large, open double window in the rear, two or three steps leading up to it. Enters Allie wild and haggard with long dishevelled hair and tattered garments, and carrying a long and crooked and forked stick, looking wildly and eagerly about.]

Allie. Here—here; 'tis, here. Oh! my child; my sweet, sweet child, so cruelly torn from me. Oh! my precious baby, here it is they keep you hidden.—Keep you from me—from me, that I might know thee not, know thee never, never more, my sweet, sweet girl. But ah!—ah! I'll foil them in their fiendish cruelty. I'll save you yet me child and thou shall know again a mother's love. Ah! what is this? what is this?—[snatches up a childs dress] Oh! blessed rag and hast thou touched my precious babe? [kisses it wildly and laughs, and cries hysterically.] Oh you most favored pretty dress. [Holds it out from her and scans it eagerly.] I'll keep it! I'll keep it! I'll have ncad of it. The child it fits is my own sweet baby girl. [Put in pocket.] Ah! [half sarcasm] and this [lifting up a childs slipper from the floor, kisses it and laughs and cries insanely. when Fritz is heard in the distance,] (hisses) what's there, [puts her hand to her ear and listens intently, leaning in the direction of the sound as it grows nearer.] Oh I must be quick— I must be quick. [Fritz is heard nearer.] They come, perhaps they'll bring my child. Oh my precious child. I'll hide out side. [Goes out, Fritz enters singing.]

> Till de la he hoo, till de la he hoo,
>    With flowers to sell I come to you.
> Till de la he hoo, till de la he hoo,
>    With flowers '  :?'l I come to you.
>
> There is cowslips yellow and daises white,
>    As fresh and fair as the morning light.
> For I gathered them fresh in the morning dew,
>    Roses red and violets blue.
> Till de la he hoo, till de la he hoo,
>    With flowers to sell I come to you.
> Till de la he hoo, all de la he hoo,
>    With flowers I come to you.
>
> There's buttercups and golden red,
>    Hyacynths and tulips too,
> Jassamine, myrtle and lilies white.
>    Boquets and nose gays all for you.
> Till de la he hoo, till de la he hoo,
>    With flowers to sell I come to you.
> Till de la he hoo, till de la he hoo,
>    With flowers I come to you.

[Fritz waltzes and plays guitar with Tracy sitting astride his neck on his shoulders. She sits erect holding a basket of roses on Fritz's head, while Fritz waltzes up and down the stage, Tracy dropping the boquets about over the floor, when the basket is empty, the child descends to the floor. As Fritz sings and dances she trips lightly from one boquet to another, as Fritz waltzes near them Tracy tosses the boquets into the basket on Fritz's head.]

Fritz. Dere now Tracy you was te biggest, te purtiest and sweetest dot was in te bunch. How many vas tat you don't got sold? Von, do, dree, four, dot vas very vell, dot vas a purdy goot bishness.

Tracy. Wooky what lots of money. [Rattles coins in the basket.] Don't you think you will be rich some day?

F. Yah, Yah, [laughs] vill pearly girly, dot vas purty certain, not much. Our pank was yoost like de spring in te plum garten. Youst as the vaters gets in tere it goes a vay quick. When I gets mine moneys vat I dinks vas mine a good teal. Ten fore Fritz could invested it, Cleo says, Fritz, Tracy wants dis, and Tracy wants dat, and it vas all gone. But I vas purty rich vne I've got my one little bete a Tracy, and you vas not so poverty struk vile I vas Fritz and sell flowers and fruits.

Tracy. Aren't you my papa Fritz.

Fritz. Nine, ha ha, [laughs] dot vas do dickelsome I youst got do laugh.

T. Why, Fritz, I think you are old enough, aren't you?

F. [Laughs boisterously.] Vel, but dumplin, every man dot vas old enough don't got to be my purty leetle girls father.

T. Well I hear the little girls that buy flowers say "papa, papa" and I want to say that to, so I think I'll have you for my papa.

F. Nine, nine me pet, dot wouldn't do.

T. Why?

F. Ha ha, [laughs ] I vas don't been too purty enough.

T. When will you be my papa?

F. Ven dere little roses commence to grow on te Jimson vead stalk, or the appricots grow on te gum tree.

T. Well, who is my papa anyhow then, if you aren't ?

F. Vell I guess you vas like all te utter sweet little girls vat dere mutbers gots. I youst guess St. Beter sent you down by delephone. [All this time Fritz has been counting his money, and now he begins deviding it ] Tere vas a time for Cleo, and tere was a quvarter for Tracy, and tere vas a nickel for Fritz, and tere was a quvarter for Cleo, and tere was a half taller for Tracy, and tere was a time for Fritz, tere was do times for Cleo, and dree times for Tracy, and one time for Fritz, and tere was a nickel for Cleo, and tere vas one time for Tracy, and tere vas nothings for Fritz.

[Tracy holds her coins in hands, Fritz puts his in his pocket, and Cleo's remain on the table.]

T.  Fritz, I meant to tell you, but since early dawn I've scarcely had time to think of it.  I had last night such a wonderful, wonderful dream.

F.  Vat vas dat tream little angel?

T.  Listen [steps to middle of the stage declaims with suitable gestures.]

It was a strange, strange dream I had last night,
    As I lay in my trundle bed;
With one little hand on my brest just so,
  , And the other beneath my head.
Some part of my dream was hard and bad,
    And made me shudder and sigh.
When I think of it now it pains my heart,
    And almost makes me cry.
But Fritz, oh Fritz, the rest of my dream,
    Was beautiful bright and sweet.
It made me think of the light of heaven,
    On the beautiful golden street.
But who do you think I thought I saw,
    In this vision that came to me.
That made me tremble anon with fear.
    Then shout with such ecstacy?
Well, I dreamed I saw my mama,
    A mama real and true—
Not some kind, sweet, make believe mama,
Just like Cleo and you,
    But my own sweet, sure enough mama,
As I've seen with the other girls.
    To kiss my sweet lips and caress me,
To smooth down my silken curls.
    When she first came before me, oh dear;
My little breast heaves with sighs,
    Her gaze was weird and excited,
Wild and sad her great big eyes,
    Her long hair hung loose and entangled,
Her garments were ragged and worn,
    Her lips stood apart as she gasped for breath,
Her bear feet were bleading and torn,
    Her thin nostrals distended—eyes a blaze,
Her long bony fingers clutched wild.
    The spell was broken—she bounded at me,
Shreiking aloud, "my child! my child!"

F.  Ouche; Tracy, dot was a big supper you eat last night.  You don't ought to have some dreams got you down on your back like dat.  You vas mate me right skeered.  I dole you, you don't got some muthers, dot maniac vomans vat vas so shlim, and don't vas comb her hair, vat don't got some shoes on, don't got some sweet lit-

tle gals like you. I youst dole you. Tracy. you don't got some mama. except me u..less it vas Cleo. Come here [takes Tracy on his
knee.]

T.   Tell me a story, Fritz, a pretty, real story. Not a may-be tale.

F.   Vat aboud I dole you Tracy.

T.   Anything so it is a true story.

F.   Vell, I youst tl ink me. I dinks I'll tole you about a lit le papy
dot would been my little sister if she done been dead. Don't I vas
tole you bout dat already. Vell I dinks n.t. Dot vas my little
sister, she vas a purty . child mit shiney plack hair and eys. She
vas name Tracy youst like you and dots vat I call you Tracy for.
Vell. my muther. dot vas Tracy's muther. I vasn't borned yet. but
heard them spoken of it. Tracy vas older as me one year. Vell.
one evening in te dark ven te lightening bugs vas youst beginin to
strike tere matches and the skeeters vas youst vaken up I guess
from ter aiternoon shleep, dot is if they ever shleep any— I don't
dinks she to Katrine. dot vas my nurse and vas been Tracy's, she
vas a big stond vomans you-t like a man. She vas took my little sister out vat vas goin to been ven I vas been borned, and make his little
planket on him bout and valked out for a stroll on te river banks
by te road. Ven the got pretty far from te house, she say as how
too mans come down a long in a horse and buggy.

T.   Just in a buggy. Fritz, drawn by a horse.

F.   Driving aloug in a horse and buggy, dot vot I say, and von
vas black and von was white.

T.   They had two horses, then—a white one and a black one.

F.   Nine. nine! Just dwo mans in von horse and buggy, and
I tole you von was white and te utter vas black.

T.   Oh, yes: the horse was white, hitched to a black buggy.

F.   Tracy, don you got some dwo cent in your head? I just
tole you dot in te horse and buggy vas dwo mans, and von was a
white mans and te utter vas a neeger. Ven te droves by Katrine
mit te leetle baby, te make der eyes at em straight quick. She notice dot and purdy soon te white gentleman just make dot tarkey
got oud from te buggy and told him tell Kathrine he wanted to
spokes mit her, and te neegar would just hold to leetle gal vile
Kathrine let te gentleman talk some sweet words or somethings
like dot te her, and ven he quit spoken and Kathrine vent to takes
some steps pack to vere she left te baby mit ter colored mans, te
mans vas gone and she run- to tole te mans in some buggies and he
vas gone. And vhat you tinks? Vile she vas listes to dem purty
words of dot man vas telling her lies bout she vas so goot looking,
te nigger just slips avay around and hid in some tick shady trees,

and ven his master come up te all got someselves in te buggy and road off mit te leetle baby. and Kathrine comed home mitout te chile (cries) and mitout von leetle sister vhat vas going to been mine. Ond vasn't dot pad?

T. Oh, dear, dear! and didn't you never hear of the child again?

F. Nine. Father thought by te neggar dot te vas from America, and I vas just going te keep looking until I find her if she been in this country.

T. That was a beautiful story, only it makes me so sad. Frits, I do hope you will find your sister. Say, Frits, what kin is she to me?

F. If I dou find her I dinks she vas been some purty far off kin.

T. I Hope, Frits, you will find her.

F. Yes, I hope so, too, but you vas gotten shleepy. I dink you dake some naps of shleep you would feel better. You vas up mit te lark tis market tay.

T. Yes, Frits, I wish you'd sing me to sleep. (Frits takes Tracy and singing a German lulaby "Rock a by." &c., pets her and places her gracefully in a hammock swung across one corner of the room and arranges the boquets around her to make a pretty picture; then waltzes and sings and sways hammock back and forth; Tracy lays with one hand under her head and one hand on her breast.)

F. Tere, now; shleep pritty creature, schleep. I just wonder why Cleo done been come back home already. It vas a good wile she don't been here quick. I done like to leave Tracy mit no somebodys here mit just but herself. Cleo just made me so mate. I wonter she don't come, when she knows I was been purty busy in te garden. (Puts on a large apron and broadbrimed straw hat; ties hat on with strings.) Vell, 'Rest purty durdle doves rest in dot shveet leetle nest," while I weed out the beautiful flowers in te garden. (Kisses his hand to Tracy and goes out.)

T. (In a low voice Tracy murmurs.) Mamma mamma! (Allie steals in, step by step, from the same end of stage the hammock swings in. She does not perceive it; looks wildly about.)

A. Where is she? Where have they hid hear? Was she not but just here this moment? Where is my child, where, where? (Col. Brance here is seen to walk apast the open window and stopping looks in unseen by Allie, and hides outside the window.) Did I not hear the music of thy enchanting voice but now? Oh, where? (Here she turns around in the act of wringing her hands when her eyes fall on the child in the hammock on which she gazes enrapped with ecstacy for an instant, then springs at the child, exclaiming,) My child, my child!

T. (Simultaneously springs up.) Mamma, mamma! (Allie catches up Tracy and tries to escape, but Col. B., who leaps in through the window, his head and person too much inveloped in an immence cape to be recognized by Allie, he snatches the child from her amidst the screams of each'; Allie, unheading the commands of her father to desist from her ravings is rudely struck to the floor, and Brance is on the eve of leaving the room with the child but is met in the door by Frits, at sight of whom Tracy cries) Frits, Frits! Save me!

F. Git oud! Git oud! you varments (snatches Tracy and knocks Branch down). Dish house done do some business like dot!

T. Fritz, I've found the mamma, I saw her in my strange dreams—there she on the floor dead! dead! Oh dear (cries).

F. Hush, Tracy, hush! You makes me mate some. Dot's nobodys but old Pranch's lunatic daughter. I heard dish morning at te market how she had escaped from te sylum mit no brains at all and less clothes. You mustn't say dot vas your mutter. Peoples tinks you vas you vas peculiar.

T. I wish Cleo would come.

F. Yes, confound Cleo. Now, Johnny-jump-up, you just go to your leetle ped and go to shleep again. (Tracy goes out. Fritz walks up to Branch and stirs him with his foot.) Here, vake up and skip mit out paying your bill. (Branch doesn't stir.) Py cho, I guess dot vot a silent partner. (Kicks Branch.) Mine Got! Vell, if he vas dead I done know if I swone it was selftefence or momuntary insanity that killed him (Stoops down and examins him.) Vell, I done know if he vas extrastink or not. I just telephone to know if his soul vas gone to hell. (Kicks him again, harder—calls aloud.) Hello-o-o, Belsepub! (Puts his hand to his ear as if holding a telephone instrument.) Hello, Primstone! Vas tish Brimstone? Yes. Vell, vas old Belsepub in? Yes. Vell, was old Branch down tere? Nine? Vell (to himself) if he vas he vas a putty shallow Branch; I just guess he vas tried up. I just vet him up a leetle (takes bucket of water and dashes it in his face.)

B. (Jumping to a sitting posture.) Whew! Whew!

F. Hello, Mr. Branch, you didn't taught you vas a limb on te tree of life to blossom in beaven already did you?

B. Oh, oh! Where am I?

F. Vell, you know you vasn't in hell or you wouldn't been so wet [kicks him] get up, get up Mishter Frogpond.

B. [Arising] Surrah! my name is Brance!

F. Mine got, you vas a mutty branch, I done know of you vas fuller of shtagnant vater and bad wiskey? Tere you did not got to steele mine purty little gal. I guess I won't knock you down of you steels dot crazy gal dot vas your own.

B. How dare you speak thus of my poor demented child.

F. Vat I got to do mit her dementled. She came of te temontaled Branch. Take off your tead plunder I say!

B. . I swear I ll not endure this. Here Gabrial here! [Branch draws a revolvar as Grbrial comes in, Fritz walks up and snatches the revolvar from Branch's hand.]

F. Tere now, angel of midnight, youst dake off dot shleeping beauty. Histe your wings and fly mit her.

B. [Going to Allie,] Allie, my child, don't you know me.

F. You vasen't so anxious for her to recognize dot elengated phis when you vas had dot cloak on your head.

B. Take her up Gabrial, be careful now.

F. Yes, dake her up denderly, handle her mitcare. Tere geminy chrismas, how she'' willrare.

G. Mars, am she dead? I bees feared to tech a dead somebodies.

F. Nine, she done been, dead,she youst been some trances. I vakes her [points pistol at Gabrial who jumps and Mr. Branch steps forward when Fritz fires at him, he fires at one then the other and general confusion reigns when Allie arouses gradually, and sits resting on one hand and runs the fingers of the other hand through her hair, then in a measured subdued voice.]

A. And—is—this—hell?

F. Nine, vomans, you vas misstooken [pointing to G.] tere vas te angel Gabrial, and tere [pointing to B.] vas te devil, but tish vas not hell ten, dish vas ven I stays. You don't seen me tid you? You tink you vas in heaven, look vat a pretty leetle cherub [struts and flaps his arms like wings.]

B. Come, Allie darling, don't you know me? Assist her to arrise Gabrial! Allie look at me, don't you know your dear father?

A. [Looks at him and seems embarrassed. She recognizes him for the first time.] Oh, ah, yes [smiles sillyly.] Why papa, papa you here?

B. Yes, my dear, aren't you going home with me?

A. Yes—yes—oh, dear—to be sure, where should I go? [Oh' my child, my child! [They are about to go out, when she turns around to Fritz.] I yet shall find my child and claim my own.

F. I vish you some good lucks. Of you fints your own ten you wont be so straight after mine. I vonters of she got some children. Dot vas curious boud Tracy's dream, I youst vonder; nine,

nine, it cannot been. Vell, I must make mine weeds out of mine garten. [Picks up garden rake and waltzes out balancing the end of the rake on his fingers. Entres Cleo and Galbraith.]

C. And so you are home from Europe once more? I'am delighted to see you.

G. Are you indeed Cleo?

C Yes indeed, Did you have a pleasant time? What sights you must have seen. Come sit down and tell of them, [they sit.] I suppose you must feel very wise now, did you learn a great deal?

G. Not so wise but I did gain some very valuable information concerning you Cleo.

C. Which concerns me, oh how ridiculous, [laughs.] Do not jest.

B. Believe me Cleo I do not jest. I speak the truth, I gained information concerning you in Europe, that is I got the information here and had it substantiated in Germany.

C. Dear me are you in earnest, you quite surprise me. What is this wonderful news? Pray tell me.

G. Very well after a little preface, I will. Do you remember Cleo, the argument advanced against our marrying was that you were an octoroon and I was a white man. Well suppose I told you you were entirely white would you marry me then?

C. No! I'd call you a liar and accuse you of trying to deceive me basely only to accomplish your purpose and thus render me miserable for life.

G. Cleo! Cleo! You do me injustice, a gross injustice. You are a white woman and I not only say it but can prove it to you beyond a doubt.

C. I don't believe you.

G. Well listen Cleo if I prove it will you marry me!

C. But I have always loved some one else.

G. You always *have*. I am to hope you don't now?

C. You need have no vain hopes about anything concerning me.

G. How unfair you are Cleo. I would have married you before I knew you were not a colored woman had you been willing, while I know, that you were supposed to be a colored woman, was the reason Branch gave to put you off.

C. Well lets hear your evidence that I am white.

G Well is it agreed? You want to know how well I love you Cleo?

C. Lets hear your story.

G. Well don't think by gaining the information I can give you that the obstacle is removed from between you and Uncle Rostund, from what I have just learned *he has known all the time.*

C. *He hasn't!* Mr. Galtraith if I was a *white* woman I'd kill you for that taunt.

G. I do not mean to taunt you Cleo, I only want to show you how foolish it is to attach anything worth while to that old rascal, who loves that old Miss Harriett Simmons and her little for unc far better than he ever did you. I am excusable for seeming egotism, but Cleo I am young, of good f mily, have some property and I hope I am as good looking as old man Branch.

C. Pray don't be so tiresome, go on with the mythical tale of my romantic babyhood.

G. Very well. Come here Uncle Paul. [A very respectable looking mulatto with snow white head comes in.] Now Cleo Uncle Paul whom you have always loved and honored and whose word you cannot doubt will bear witness to every thing I say.

P. Yes Honey, Mr. Tom. will only speak de truf.

C. Oh dear you all quite unnerved me.

T. Cleo, as you know from childhood as we grew up together, i learned to love you and when I became old enough to understand it my heart was broken because as I thought you were colored we could not marry. But as you know I came to love you so ardently and from Allie's going insane I was relieved from my obligations to her and could not be deprived of my heritage for not marrying her, that I resolved to marry you if you were an octoroon, you know how you refused repeatedly saying I would repent of my bargain. I was so disappointed and wished so much that you were really white and the obstacle thus removed, that I began to hope it might be really true, and with this faint hope I consulted Uncle Paul about it and questioned him so closely that he would not take an oath that he knew you to be really as you were supposed to be an octoroon. This gave me some encouragement. I questioned him until, to satisfy me and to relieve a guilty conscience, he owned to me that the real Cleo *born* to Aunt Kizzy was through his carelessness drowned in the Danube river and to satiate Uncle Rostund's terrible wrath he stole you from your nurse while traveling in Germany and presented you to him in the place of the child that was drowned. Aunt Kizzy agreed to and did raise you as her child. All the particulars Uncle Paul will give you in time, sufficient to say I took the articles he stole with you, this blanket, this little dress and most of all, this little locket with the two pictures in it and went to Germany with them and learned without a doubt that all he said was true.

Cleo. Daddy Paul is this *true?*

P.  True as de gospel of de Lord.

C.  And Mammy Kizzy was not my own mother.  How strange it all seems.  Well what of my real parents, Mr. Galbraith?

G.  Your parents are of the German gentry.  Count Frederick your father and Countess Theressa your mother.  Your mother is dead, and your father still lives.

C.  Mr. Galbraith I am unable to express my gratitude, my feeling.  Leave me to myself, let me think.

G.  What I have done is all I could, but it is little compared to what I ask in return.  But I shall hope that you will think of me kindly and all I have done.

C.  I shall indeed.

G.  Thank you dear Cleo.  Good morning, I shall call again this evening, I hope you will not think me too impatient.

C.  Good by.  Very well I'll expect you.  [Exit G. and P.]

Cleo.  Oh fool, fool, what a fool I have been to help to so deceive poor Allie Branch and then to be so deceived myself.  [Takes basket of unironed clothes from closet and begins sprinkling preparatory to ironing.]  I might have known that a man who could have been so cruel to his daughter could be no kinder to poor wretched me.  [Some one knocks gently at the outer door.  Cleo. listens.  B. without.]

B.  Cleo!

C.  Is that you Master Rostand.  Why don't you come in? it seems to me you are unusually timid just now.

B.  [Peeping in.]  Is Fritz here?

C.  No, and if he were, what's the difference? he would not object to your being here, and if he did isn't this my house?

B.  [Coming in.]  That's true, I had not thought of it.  I tried to intercept you before you got here, I wanted some little private business with you.

C.  Why don't you want to come where Fritz is?

B.  Ahem!  I know better than I can tell you.

C.  Well I shouldn't have stopped until I got home if you had overtaken me.  What is it you want?

B.  Do you know Allie has escaped again from the asylum?

C.  Yes I just now heard it.

B.  Well it makes things very disagreeable for me.

C.  Any more so now than on former occasions?

B.  Well yes, she still has an idea that this child here is hers and says so, so repeatedly and with such emphasis that I find that it is becoming the impression of many that it is her child.

C. Well?

B. Cleo something must be done.

C. And as usual I must do it. Which one do you want me to kill, Allie or the child?

B. Not so bad as that.

C. What then?

B. I have the papers here all right, all you will have to do is to sign your name, I will witness it. I want you to make affidavit that the child is yours by birth?

C. I would not do it to save your life, no not to save your soul from perdition.

B. Be careful what you say Cleo. You remember the terms of our contract was that you were to destroy the identity of the child. It has not been done yet.

C. It is done as effectually as I can do it or ever will do it,

B. It has not been done at all. Do you know what but just now transpired in this house of yours.

C. No! What?

B. Allie came here and got the child and but that I intercepted her and took the the child away from her she would have escaped with it. She avowed it was her child, and what is stranger still the child declared she knew Allie was her mama.

C. She did! poor thing! poor thing! and is it to this I put my hand.

B. Now how easily this impression that the child is Allie's could be squelched if you would but swear that the child is yours.

C. You heard what I said?

B. But that can't be final?

C. As final as the day of judgment. You hear me?

B. Then you must consider our engagement broken.

C. [Laughs derisively.] Our engagement?

B. Yes, our engagment!

C. Which one, you know we have two? One that I'm to do your clear starching and also that I'm to do your ironing. Now which one shall be cancelled?

B. You know what I mean, Cleo; unless you sign this paper I shall consider myself under no obligations to be true to my oath to you.

C. You are under no such obligations anyhow. You are as free as a crow in a corn field.

B. Then you won't sign this paper?

C. I'd see you writhe in the very bowels of torment first.

B. Then I'll make you sign it. [Arises and spreads paper out on the table, places ink and pen and walkes up to Cleo.] Now sign that paper?

C.   I won't, I won't.  [B. attempts to take hold of her when she throws the water in the pan in his face.  He steps backward and recovers himself from the shock of the water, then steps suddenly toward her with his fist drawn to strike her.  Gleo confronts him boldly.]  Strike me if you dare, you cowardly puppy!  Strike a woman!  [B. hesitates.]

B.   [Meekly.]  Cleo do you love me no more?

C.   Love you!  Love you?  I despise you!  I loath you!  Poor fool that I was to think you were worthy of my notice.

B.   You indeed, who are you to talk to me thus.  Born in slavery, where your mother writhed under the master's lash.  Whose very fore-fathers fattened on human flesh in the wilds of Africa.

C.   [Confronting him and shaking her fist in his face.]  Y-o-u i-i-e!

B.   Who was your mother but the slave woman Kiziah?  *Who indeed was your mother?*

C.   Countess Theressa!

B.   Ha! ha!  [laughs scornfully and walks back a pace and then turns and walks up to Cleo abruptly.]  See here Cleo, lets done with all this nonsence.  Sign that paper!  Do you hear me?

C.   [Walks and opens the door.]  There!  [Points to the door.]  *Leave my house,* you infamous dog!

B.   Sign that paper or I'll choke you.  [Catches her and chokes her, and thursts her down on to her knees, as she clutches at his wrists, and gasps.  Fritz enters with a basket of big red apples and seeing the situation, throws one striking Branch in the head, who releases Cleo and claps his hands to his head, while Fritz continues pelting him with the apples, as they race around the room.]

F.   Git oud, you youst hants mine house like some unclean spirits.  [Cleo stands and laughs and claps her hands as Fritz hurls the last apple at Branch, impulsingly sails the empty basket at Cleo, lodging it on her head, and simultaneously he grabs up first B's cloak and then his hat and hurls them at him as he escapes through the window.  Then he rushes at Cleo with the exclamation.]

F.   Gleo vene agin sometime you grossed dot crooked creeks vid dot mutty banks vat you been stuck in?

C.   Shut your mouth!

F.   I wish you youst keep dot man avay from here, I dole you.

C.   Indeed I guess I'll allow who I please to come to my house.

F.   You von't!

C.   I will!

F.   You shan't I tell you.

C.   I shall I tell you, there now take that.  [Hits him with the basket. Cleo cries and Fritz rushes at her but instead of hitting her goes on a past her,]

F. Mine Got I'm youst goin to busht up this partnership business and run a shepang of my own.

C. Well bust up then you old fat red faced dutchman!

F. Confound you I vill you old shlim yaller faced nigger!

C. [Burst into a flood of tears.] I'm not a yellow faced nigger.

F. [Cries too.] I'm not a red faced dutchman. [Cleo sits down and cries.] Boo—hoo, I'm youst going to go off from here. Boo—hoo—so I am—boo—hoo. [Aside smiling.] She tinks I'm in earnest. Cleo, you Cleo-o-o, I vas youst goin to leave here. [Cleo does not heed him.] Boo—hoo. [Cries, walks on toward the door expecting Cleo to ask him not to go.] Boo—hoo, goot by Gleo, I'm going to join the regulars, boo—hoo—.

C. Well go off and join the regulars. I hope you don't think I care.

F. Boo—hoo, [cries boistrously, comes up to her and makes an effecting good by.] Goot by, goot by, I vas ben goot to you and you vas most been goot to me, boo—hoo, you youst been evryting to me, my friend, my—my—sister, and mine—mine—muther inlaws.

C. Mother-in-law! What do you mean,? Go off from me!

F. I mean you vas youst goot to me like somepodies dot vasn't mine muthers.

Boo—hoo, wen you hears I vas shot, [aside.] She don't know tere vas no wars. [aloud.] When you hears I vas shot you youst trop one little tear on my lonely grave vat no podies can't find and I vill forgive you, goot by. [Cleo cries.] [a side.] I vas youst a foolin her. I youst hide and hear vat she says wen she tinks I'm gone. [To C.] Vell goot by, boo—hoo, goot by Cleo. You shveet good angel you. [Fritz goes out, then slips in, as Cleo keeps on crying.)

C. Oh dear I am so lonely I wish he would come back, I wish he would come back! I'm so lonely here without him, [aside.] Noble Tom Galbraith. [aloud.] I talked to harsh to him after he had been so kind. But I know he'll come back again, he'll come again.

F. (Aside.) Here dot, youst hear dot, she's comming around all right.

C. (Sobbing.) He has been my best, best friend, and we shall yet live happily together.

F. (Aside.) You pet, I'd youst tie for Cleo, and youst goin to tell her.

C. And Branch! old Rostand Branch! Bah! I despize him! I

despise him! I could grind his heart beneath my heal. Oh (cries) it frightens me to think what a narrow escape I had. (Aside. What if I had married him. (Aloud.) What a narrow escape, indeed. It frightens me to tears to think of it. (Cries.) And if what he said be true I have no room to call Fritz dutch. Oh dear I wish he'd come back. (Cries. Fritz has sliped unobserved to 'o her back and lays his hand on her shoulder.)

F. Tere now Cleo don't cry dot vay I vasn't goin off to te var.

C. (Cries aloud.) I know that you old fool you that's why I am crying. Go off from me!

F. I von't done it, I von't now by golly!

C. Go off from me to the army and get shot, you red faced dutchman!

F. I von't, I von't get shot if I go to te army, I youst lay up in some parracks, and eat and shleep and traw my pay.

C. Well, go off from here, I say!

F. Vat you say you vas lonely mitoud me, and you wish I'd come pack?

C. Were you evesdropping me, you scamp? thats like you, you unprincipled rascal! Lonely without you, iudeed, dear me, I hope you didn't think I meant you, did you? Well I didn't!

F. You didn't! Vell, who did you mean? You didn't mean Mr. Pranch, for you said, you tespished him.

C. Well, I declare, lonely without you! You don't know who you are talking to, I guess I meant Mr. Tom. Galbraith, that's who i meant, a gentleman.

F. And vasn't I! Of you tink so high of him, vat you tink of me?

C. (Walks up to him and slaps him in the face.) Thats what I think of you! (She runs to the opposite end of the room. Fritz i cks up one of the apples, from the floor and hurls it at Cleo, bare-y missing Tracy, who runs in between them catching the hand of Fritz.)

T. Oh! I'm so pleased to find you both in such a good humor, don't let me interrupt you. Come go on petting Cleo, Fritz! (Pulls F. who steps a step or two, nearer Cleo. Tracy then goes to Cleo, and pulls her a step or two nearer Fritz. She goes from one to the other, pulling them nearer and nearer, they approached with seeming reluctance, casting furtive glances at each other, until they are both near Tracy, who stands between them on a stool, which she has placed between them.)

T. Now kiss me papa Fritz, (he kisses her.) Now kiss me mama Cleo, (she kisses her.) Now both kiss me at once, (they hes-

itate.) Now when I say three, kiss me both at once, one—two—
quick now--three, (as she says three, she jumps back out of th
way, and Fritz, and Cleo, kiss one another, and Tracy, runs out of
the room.)

F.   (Shyly.)  Vas dot a plunder buss, Cleo?

C.   (Modestly.)  It must have been a minky buss, if you kissed
a nigger.

F.   I didn't a kiss a nigger, I kissed a nice lady.  (They are silent a moment, as Fritz stands looking at her.)  Vat did you kiss
Cleo?

C.   I kissed a German.

F.   Does he got some red faces and fat?

C.   Not very!  Thats not so bad.

F.   Dot's a purty girl, lets take a leetle tance.  (They waltz and
ballance up and down the stage, and Fritz, sings snatches of some
German love song.  They sit down.)

F.   Cleo, do you love me?

C.   Why yes, of course Fritz!

F.   How much?

C.   More than tongue can tell.

F.   Whoo-pe, Cleo, you make me so happy!

C.   But Fritz, I—I—only love you as a brother.  (Fritz, turns
his back to her.)  You know Fritz, I'm older than you, I could not
love you any other way, could I?

F.   I thought you might—might—been my—my mother-in-law.

C.   Ha! ha! say Fritz, what did you get so mad at me for, after
you had run old man Rostand away?

F.   Vhot you don't stay avay from some places quicker, and
been home sooner?  Ten vat you vants mit old Pranch, ven I youst
trove him oud of my house, a vile ago, ven he tried to steal Tracy?

C.   I came as quick as I could, but I had not seen Master Rostand, he came here.

F.   Say Cleo, vasn't you stuck on that shanks yet?

C.   Stuck on him, no, I despise him!

F.   Vat vas that about you and Mr. Galbrath, vat you vas
sohloquizing?

C.   (Embarrassed.)  Oh! don't ask me Fritz!

F.   Oh! now Cleo!

C.   Well, you don't care do you?

F.   Don't care for what?

C.   Well—well, Fritz we're engaged, Mr. Galbraith, and me.

F.   Vat vas dot, vas you and him goin into some business together?

C. Well, yes we are going to get married. And oh! Fritz, I'll have such a fine elegant house, to live in, for you know Mr. Galbrath, is a very wealthy man.

F. I thought of he don't married his cousin Allie, he don't somethings got?

C. Yes, but Allie's going insane did away with all that, and now he comes into posession of everything, and I shall be mistress of Galbrath Hall, just think of that Fritz, won't that be splendid, I am just delighted. I can scarcely realize it, that elegant stone mansion, with its stately columns, wide halls and beautiful drawing rooms. Oh! Frits, I'm just wild with ecstacy. [Frits, don't seem pleased.] Why Frits, why don't you rejoice with me? Aren't you glad?

F. Nine, nine.

C. Now, Frits, don't be selfish, and envious. I'm tired of being so poor.

F. You youst might have waited to left me, ven Tracy was been bigger, I vish I'd gone one to the regulars, where I started.

C. You never started, you old goose you. Now honey, hanny, be nice and I'll tell you what I'll do.

F. Vat you done?

C. Don't you remember once, when we were short of flowers, for the fair, and Mr. Galbrath, allowed us to supply our deficiency from the gardens up there, don't you remember what elegant gardens they had there, only they were very much out of repair, and unkept, Well I'll get Mr. Galbrath, to allow you to take charge of the Galbrath gardens and orchards, and what a delightful occupation that will be, and Tracy, and you and I can all be together still. Just think of it.

F. Got pless you Cleo, you vas a whole apple cart, you vas so shveet. Hootsy cootsy pootsy. [Chuckles her under the chin.]

C. Oh! you might know I would not separate from you, as long as we have been together.

F. And Tracy vill be tere do!

C Yes, and you!

F. Yes, and you!

C. And Tracy too!

F. Yes, and me do!

C. Yes, and I too!

F. Yes, all dree of us!

C. Yes, and all three of us!

F. One, do, dree, Tracy, you and me!

C. Yes, one, two, three, Tracy, you and me!

F. Whoo-pee, whoo-pee! You, Tracy, and me!

C. Tracy, Fritz and Cleo!

F. Tracy, you and me o!

[During this dialogue they dance and kiss and frolic in ecstacy, they seem so occupied with one another, and their prospects that they do not hear a knocking outside. It is repeated louder, and louder, for several times, until, old Miss Harriet Simmons walks in unobserved by them, just as they are in the act of embracing.]

H. S. [With mock modesty.] Oh! well, did you ever, oh!

F. Hello, old silver threads among the gold! vat you vant's!

H. S. Oh! how shocking! Cleo, how dare you allow this ruffian address me in this manner, so unbecoming and foreign to one in my high position?

C. I'm out of that thing. (Goes out.)

H. S. Oh! but stay, stay Cleo, Cleo!

C. (From outside.) *Excuse me Miss Harriet!*

H. S. Oh! oh! alone with this bear, oh! dear; what shall I do alone with this *bear*.

F. Say romans, you vas mishtooken-; tish vas a flower gardens; it vasn't a zoological gardens, unless you vas come to been te monkey.

H. S. Oh! what shall I do! where can I escape?

F. You forgot mighty quick, tere vas te toor vat come in you at.

H. S. [Imploring him.] Have you no mercy? Pitty a poor young damsel.

F. Tid you say young?

H. S. The dew of the morning, scarce dried from my lips!'

F. Chew of te morning?

H. The rose bloom of spring yet fresh on my cheeks!

F. Fresh on your cheeks?

H. Oh! have you no heart? The lion could but tear me to pieces, the cannibals but eat me alive, and the—

F. Bear could but hug you, (hugs her, she screams and falls almost fainting in his arms.)

H. My smelling salts quick, there I feel better. (Frits eases her down onto a sofa.)

F. Tere now you she giraff, what for you come to te bears' den.

H. Ah! now Mr. Frit,z how can you speak of me so unkindly. (streches her neck,) I'm sure my neck is none to long.

F. Oh! now Miss Harriet, how come you speke so unkindly, I'm sure I'm not so bear.

H. Ha! ha! how amusing! really you are quite entertaining,

come sit down, arn't you tired standing? One can converse so much more pleasantly when seated closely together.

F. Dot vas true; you can carry on a conversation by himself, he just stay as close mit himself as he want to. Your skin and bones was purty close. But ven two wants to converse, and dot vas you and me, it vas youst as more agreeable to don't ben as close.

H. (Jumping up.) What do you mean?

F. Oxcuse me; noddings, nodding, I youst mean you vas some older as te day you vas born.

H. Skin and bones, indeed!

F. Yah! Of you mean you don't got some skin and bones you vas in some bad fixes.

H. S. Oh, you hush, you old heathen dutchman!

F. Say, old romans, go git somepodies to lay you avay on te shelf, you vas tamag_d goods.

H. S. Damaged! damaged! I'm not damaged.

F. If you vasn't so *damn aged*, you vasn't so tam young.

H. S. I shall tell my husband of this insult.

F. Your husband?

H. S. Yes my husband.

F. I dinks te oldest settlers done forgot ven you vas married.

H. S. Hear the peddler! I was married but just this day—just now,

F. Oh, I forgot cherries vas ripe. I guess somebody vants to set up skee-crow.

H. S. I'll pay you for your impudence. I came here for ten baskets of flowers, and now I won t take but two, I want two baskets of flowers.

F. Say, vat old man took you for a muskeeto bars—to keep te skeeters away o'nights.

H. If you mean who is my husband (with a courtesy,) I am the young and blushing bride of Col. Rostund Branch. Oh, Fritz, it was so romantic! You see, my father——

F. Before he died.

H. He's been dead a few years.

F. About fifty, I think.

H. Well, perhaps; but as I was saying, he never approved of my marrying a poor man. Well, if Mr. Branch is aristocratic, I think he is poor—that is, he has plenty but not so rich as I am, and so—and so—

F. You shveet leetle young goslings, whose fatter been tead sixty years, thought you'd have a runavay scrape, tid you?

H. No, but I thought as papa was opposed to my marrying a

poor man, I was afraid if I deliberated something might happen to pursuade me not to have him, and so when he and the squire rode up to call on me, and named it, I just slipped into my low-necked and short-sleeved dress, and had the ceremony performed right then and there. Oh, dear, it's quite overcome me, Mr. Fritz (effects embarrassment), and one so young will blush at such tender reference. Oh, I'm a bonny bride! [Hides her face behind her fan.]

F. Yhaw. Yhaw (laughs). If you vas a bride at all you vas a bony one. [Pulls fan away] Ten you and old Branch vas tied togetter, vash you?

H. Yes, the knot has been tied.

F. You vas Mr. and Mrs. Branch. Your children vould been well ropes.

H. Oh, how shocking you talk! I'm just going out to the garden where Cleo is.

F. Vell, you said you vanted ten baskets of flowers, tid you?

H Yes, to decorate my house with. [Exit Harriet.]

F. Dot old duck don't shwim so vell mit dot Branch as she tinks. He joust got her for her money and ven he run drough mit dot he youst died mit old age, or run avay mit a vomans vat vas better as lookin. I vonder vat made him been so sutten? [Knocking.] Hello, who vash dot? Come in! [Two officers enter.] Hello, Messrs. Come-along. [He picks up two apples from the floor] Tere vas no innocent vidows and orphans here for you to take instead of the vicked men vat you always lets git avay. [Tosses the apples up, one after the other, catching them.]

1st Officer. Well. see here, dutchy, don't you be so smart. We have come after somebody here. [Frits, not heeding, keeps ou tossing the apples and dancing.] Say, is there no one here but you? [Frits still ignores him.] Say, can't you understand English? [Frits, without stopping dancing instantaneously, throws each of the two apples striking eachot the two officers who fall backwards.]

F. Can't you understand dutch? [Laughs at them as they arise.] Now, vat you vants here?

1st O. We have come to arrest somebody.

F. Who you vants to arrest? I'm not tead and you know Frits vas never taken alive yet. Every time they took me they took me tead.

2d O. How many times have been taken?

F. [Throwing apple and striking 2d officer in the stomach from the effects of which he bends double.] There, that's twice you been taken.

1ts O. Look here, let's have done with this nonsense. We are the officers of the law and must be obeyed. We have come to secure the insane daughter of Col. Branch, who we are informed is here in your residence.

F. She is not here; vat you tinks I want mit old Branch's lunatics daughter?

1st. O. She has some strange hallucination that the child, Tracy. you have here is her daughter. It is strange if she is not here, she was seen to come this way but just now. She is not here then?

F. Nine, she vasn't here ten nor now either.

1st. O. Well, my friend, we will be obliged to search your house thoroughly, otherwise we will not be discharging our duty.

F. All right, I youst tole you dot whisky in te cellar has got sticnine in it, so you'd better not steal any. [The men start as if to search. Frits says, aside,] I dought of sometings. [Laughs.] I youst play a joke. I youst put em on te old man's bride. She youst almost as crazy as his daughter. [Aloud.] Say, look here, you fellows, vat draws your pay, vould you know dot vomans of you seen her?

1st. O. Well, the old man gave us a minute description of her; perhaps we might recognize her.

F. You never have seen her?

1st. O. No, she is described to us as being very spare. with hair sprinkled with gray.

F. Vel, I said she's not here, vasn't, but I say now dot she has been here, of she vas now or not I don't know. She says she wanted some flowers, and she went to the garden.

2nd. O. Why didn't you tell us this at first?

F. Vell, you never vants to arrest no podish and I th ught may be of I help you out of this by saying she vasn't here, you'd give me a rebate on somethings like dot, but ven I saw you vas goin to search, I thought I youst' save you te troubles. I youst call her. (Aside.) Dots purty good. (Goes to the door, then turns back.) Say, you fellows vat talks to the servant girl in the back gate, vile the rogue gets away out te front. Say, tis vomans has another hell-of-a-loose-notion, or what ever you call it.

O. Hallucination. What is it?

F. Vell, it vas a hell of a loose nation, vat got you to do cus todian business, but say, tish vomans has a notion vat she will tell you, dot is she says she is Col. Branch's bride, his wife. [Goes out.]

1st. O. That's it, that's what he said she'd say, she thinks she is Branch's wife.

2nd. O. Strange isn't it? What else did he say of her?

1st. O. In accordance with the notion that she is Col. Branch's bride, she insists on wearing on all occasions an evening dress.

2nd. O. He said also, that she insists on coming to this vender of flowers, for flowers to adorn the brides chamber.

1st. O. Says also, she is very tall like himself and although not naturally so has become very much emaciated, and looks much older than she really is.

2nd. O. Insists also, that Squire Jones, performed her marriage ceremony.

F. (Enters laughing.) Here spring chicken, here are the gentlemens vat wants to see you safe home.

H. Oh, ah, strangers! Oh, ah, I—I thought it was my dear husband and the squire.

Both Officers. Tis she! tis she!

1st. O. The slender form, the gray hair.

2nd. O. The evening dress, the plain gold ring.

F. There does dot fill te bill of tescription?

Both O. Exactly!

F. [To H.] Say, spring beauty, these gentleman vant's to see you safe home, to tere shveet by and by. They say you vas clean gone on te rid side out of your head. Gentleman, she vas crazy as a ped bug.

H. How dare you so traduce the name of the bride of the eminent, worthy Col. Br nch. [Slaps Fritz in the face and the first officer lays his hand on her shoulder.

1st. O. I am very sorry it is necessary madam, but I must confirm what the man says. We have come to conduct you to the asylum from whence we know you to have escaped. We know you to be Col. Branch's daughter Allie.

H. [Screams.] Oh, 'tis false! 'tis false! I am Col. Branch's bride of half an hour! oh, how dare you!

F. Oh, yes, of you dont call me a bear a vile ago, you could proves dot by me.

H. [Attempting to free herself.] Unhand me I say! unhand me! oh, you wretches!

1st. O. Be quiet lady, we shall not hurt you. You, father requests us to place you in the carriage awaiting outside.

H. My father! who? when? my father? why villian, my father's been dead these sixty years and better!

F. And te morning dews vasn't tried off your lips yet.

H. Oh, to be so humilliated and I a bride!

1st. O. How like the desription.

2nd. O. Everything verified.

F. [Laughs.] Vell, goot tay you gentlemans, vat was never on a beat; goot tay gentle Allie. [Aside, as he goes out.] Dot vas a pretty rough joke. I guess she's tough enough to bear it. She'll have plenty of goot satisfaction to pay for it, vhen they dakes her to her new husband. I youst tinks Branch vill rare and shvare vhen he sees they have caught the wrong bird. [Exit.]

1st. O. Come lady, you shall confront Mr. Branch, and if he says you are his bride and not his daughter, you shall be free to go to his arms.

H. Free to go to his arms! oh, ecstatic dream. [They lead her toward the door.]

2nd. O. Why here is Col. Branch, and the squire now.

1st. O. Indeed it is true. [They enter.]

H. [Frees herself and rushes wildly at Branch ] Oh, my husband! my darling! [B. steps back and coldly warns her off.] Oh, do not be offended at finding me in the company of these men. I could not help it, could I Fritz? Fritz! (calls, but B. remains stolid.) Am I not your wife? Did you not but just kiss my maiden lips? Am I not still your sweet young wife? (B. shakes his head and she screams, then turning to Jones.) Squire Jones, did you not but just this hour pronounce us man and wife?

Squire. I did not.

H. (Screams.) Oh, what cruel jest is this! oh, my husband, my darling, is this not my wedding ring? scarce warm upon my finger yet, since placed there from your cold, cold hands. (Takes off ring.) See, the inscription, "Rostand Branch, to his bonny bride." Who is your bonny bride but me?

B. You see, it is as I told you, you must away with her. You see the squire refutes what she says, and anyone will tell you I have been a widower these last ten years, and 'tis well known to all, the sad, sad tale of my demented daughter, so take her away.

1st. O. We understand. Here madam!

H. (Falling on her knees before Branch.) Am I so soon forsaken! Oh, my husband, my precious, precious husband! Have you no mercy?

B. Away with her I say; are you not officers of the law? Is it not as I told you? why hesitate?

1st. O. Come woman, we can but do our duty. [They assist her to arise.]

H. [With out-stretched arms she makes one last appeal to Branch.] Am I not your wife?

B. No! [She faints and falls in the arms of the officers, who bear her off.]

Squire. Remember Colonel, for my part in this dirty business, I am to have one-fourth of the woman's fortune.

B. Don't anticipate the thing is not consummated yet.

Sqr. Well I just wished to remind you of what part is mine, and you had better see that I get it.

B. I need no reminder, I shall not forget a thing so painful to me. [With a sneering laugh:] That one-fourth my wife's fortune must go to the man that made us man and wife.

Sqr. A big fee enough. But you can laugh as haughtily as you please, but you'd better see that I get **my** share.

B. Hold your peace.

Sqr. That's what I want to do—my *piece* of Miss Harriet's fortune. You'd better help me to it, too.

B. Be still; threats are quite out of place. Mrs. Branch's fortune is fifty thousand dollars. The fourth of it is twelve and a half—*your life to me,* who can take it, is not worth that sum. (Exeunt, enters F. and C.]

C. I am afraid, Fritz, to have your everlasting joke, you have gone too far this time. Its my opinion you have lent your hand to something not straight. Col. Branch is, you know, mean enough to do anything.

T. Vat you dink?

C. Well, I believe he married Miss H. rriet for her fortune, and then to get rid of her purposely sent her off to an insane asylum as his daughter.

F. Vat makes you dinks dot.

C. Listen. Branch has litterally nothing. Miss Harriett has fifty thousand dollars. It has become proverbial, and that fifty thousand dollars is an attachee of Miss Harriet's, as well understood as her long nose. Old master has told me repeatedly he could not bear the idea of living with her, but coveted her fortune.

F. Yes, but he has a lunatic daughter and she is out, for she was here to-day.

C. Certainly ; but Frits, Miss Harriet told me Col. Branch told her that Allie was safely confined in one of his second story rooms; that he had concluded not to send her back to the asylum, and his reason for the hasty wedding was because the officers in pursuit of Allie would soon be here and he wanted her safely ensconced in his house, and wanted Miss Harriet to assist him in taking charge of his additional duties, and to make it appear Allie were rightly situated, that the men might not insist on taking her back. She consented, and he sent her post haste after the flowers. That was a pretext, I think.

F.   Who would a thought dot Branch ras as deeper as dot? But vhen a branch was so mutty you couldn't tell of he vas deep or shallow.

C.   Well, Fritz, you must see to this, and if there has been any crime perpetrated you must help hunt it out and see that the criminals are properly dealt with.

F.   Dot I will, Gleo; dot Pranch ras purty dirty, but of he vas deep or shallow I wades him this time.

C.   Well, go for Tracy while I prepare dinner.  (Exit F.)  Poor Miss Harriet, to be so foully dealt with.  Her portion is much worse than mine.  One can scarcely help wishing such fiends in hell, where they belong.  Old Rostand has no idea of leaving Allie at home.  He will simply keep her here until Miss Harriet is safely confined.  To the people about here and those connected with Miss Harriet's property, he is her husband; to the asylum folks, he is not her husband.  Old Squire Jones is to testify each way, as the occasion requires.  [Enters Fritz and Tracy, both hands joined and swinging round and round, singing "Ring around a rosy, bottle full o' posy."  Cleo places a few dishes on the table from the closet, arranges a large boquet in middle of table; Frits and Tracy waltz about until Cleo has the table prepared.]  Come, the feast is made ready.  [Fritz swings Tracy into a high chair and places her at the table back; Frits and Cleo sit at opposite ends; with bowed heads; Fritz proceeds with the blessing.]

F.   Our Fatter, vat ras in heaven and everywhere else all at once and te same times; vat has been living all tish time and vas youst the same age yet; vat vas fatter to everybody else as yell as te dutchman.  Ve don't got nodings but ve thank Thee dot it vas good enough vat there vas of it, and plenty of it, sich as vas.  Bless Cleo, bless Tracy, and don't forgot Fritz, forever and ever for Christ's sake.  Amen.  [Curtain.]

———o———

## ACT III.

### (*Eleven Years Later.*)

SCENE—A large splendid drawing-room at Galbraith Hall, opening into a conservatory back—Cleo, now an elegant matron, reclining near one end of stage beside a center-table, on which stands a vase with a faded boquet, and a glass of wine.  A little boy and a twelve year old colored girl are just completing an immense tower of blocks. The topmost block is placed.

Tommy. Look mama isn't it beautiful?

C. Yes, Tommy, my son, you are quite a skillful builder. (Goes on reading.)

T. Let's catch hands and skip round it, Mary Lucy. (They join hands and skip round the tower as Fritz appears from conservatory with a broad grin on his face, and a large boquet in his hand.)

F. The last rose of summer. (Strikes his breast.) Dot vas me. (Walks up to table and observes Cleo closely, drinks the wine from the glass, removes the faded buquet and fills wine glass with water from vase.) Dot vas to Vice President of the C. W. T. U. (Points to C. who reaches for the glass and unconsciously sips the water, and makes becoming ado about it. Fritz laughs, places the boquet in vase, stands looking at Cleo a moment then throws the faded boquet, knocking her paper from her hands.)

C. Oh, Fritz, do be more dignified. When will you ever learn to be a man? I declare you are just like you were when I first knew you.

F. You vasn't just like you vere when I first knew you.

C. Why, Fritz; have I changed materially?

F. You may been to same material, but you vas changed.

C. How, Fritz, I am older I know than I was then?

F. In tem days youth vasn't your only crime.

C. What can you mean?

F. Oxcuse me, you vas a neegar then, and now you vas a white lady.

C. Oh Fritz, Fritz, how can you be so rude and unkind. (Picks up paper, in the meantime Tommy and Mary Lucy have quit skipping around the blocks and as M. L. pats, Tommy dances. Frits looks at him and begins dancing about the room. Cleo reads. Fritz purposely dances to the block tower, kicks it, scattering the blocks.)

T. Aw now, mamma look what uncle Fritz has done. (Fritz snatches Tommy up and dances out of the room with him.)

C. Mary Lucy, pick up the blocks, quick.

M. L. Yes'm. [Throws the blocks hurriedly into the box and Frits dances in and up to M. L., running her out of the room, then turns and walks to Cleo.]

F. Now, Gleo, vot vash dot you vas been goin to tole me? I youst pelieves you vas tryin to shlip oud of it. You von't talk to me all te time some times, like you used to in te cottage.

C. Yes, I do; I see you every day.

F. So tid Moses see to prom'sed land, but he tid not get to it, all te same. Seeing me vas not spoken mit me. Vat with Mr. Galbrath and te servents and tem children youst been next to you all te time, till I don't spoke to you not much.

C. Well, I am all attention, Frits; what is it?

F. Vat is it? You know it is vat, Gleo.

C. No I don't, really. What is it you wish me to tell you? Sit down, Fritz.

F. You been promising to tole me all vot I vants to know about Tracy.

C. What good would that do you, Fritz? Tracy has promised to marry you; is not that satisfactory?

F. [Laughs.] Beat study, by jirks, mine heart. [Strikes his left breast.] To been Tracy's husband vould been enough to satisfy any bodies, but you don't kill me off mit dot gun, even if I vas a goin' to marry Tracy—a man can't found oud too much dot vas true about dot vomans dat vas going to took him for better as worse as he vas.

C. That's quite true; but how much better could a man know his promised wife than you do Tracy?

F. As much better as you know her as I know her, I youst vants to know who she vas. You said her mother vas rich and ve vould got it when her mother died.

C. Well, Fritz, I am surprised. Are you so mercenary as that? I don't want any of Tracy's money were she to get it, and if you marry her and she does get it all you need not complain.

F. I youst vants to know bond it myself. Of I axes you some questions vould you shpoke mit me straight?

C. If I speak at all.

F. Vell, ten, do you know who vash Tracy's parents?

C. I do.

F. Vash te dead yet, youst now?

C. They are not.

F. Vash her fatter and mutter living togetter now?

C. I understand they are.

F. You understand? Who dole you, vas they been in this neighborhood now?

C. No, they are not here now. I know of them, as my husband, Mr Tom Ganbraith, has from time to time gotten letters from Tracy's tather.

F. Gleo, you vas don't say dot! Vas I don't never seen him?

C. Yes he has been here at our house since Tom and I were married

F.  Gleo! Whoop-ee!  Who vas dot?

C.  Fritz, if I tell you who are her parents will it make any difference in your affairs?

F.  Nine—I shwore.

C.  Well, do you remember an officer in the Federal army on the General's staff that had his headquarters at Col. Branch's house, by the name of McGregor?

F.  Dot man vat I ships in te crape myrtle bushes and he vas kissin' you like five-hundred, and you said vat made you done it vas because you favored te union so.

C.  Yes, he's the one.

F.  I tole you, vasn't you kis-in' him for Abe. Lincoln.

C.  Yes, you remember the man then.  Well that man's Tracy's father.

F.  Vas Tracy, a little yankee?

C.  Evidently, on her father's side.

F.  Look here Cleo, vas you been Tracy's mother?

C.  Ha, ha, no indeed, didn't I tell you I was of the impression Tracy's parents were living toget!er?  No Fritz, I am not the only woman McGregor kissed while the yankee general and his staff were quartered in our house.

F.  Did Col. McGregor kiss Tracy's mother while he was quartered at Branch's?

C.  I don't know, I guess so.  Now don't grasp at conclusions too hastily, Tracy's parents were marrie! in Baltimore, Maryland.

F.  Tay vas, oh, vell, I vas youst aboud to surmise somctings else.

C.  What did you surmise?

F.  Vell, she is of a good family of she did vent crazy.  I dole you Cleo, I thought you vas goin' to say Allie Branch was Tracy's muther.

C.  Well, what if I had.  She was such a sweet little woman before she became insane, and everybody admired her and love! her.  What if Tracy is Allie's child?

F.  Vell, I dole you now Cleo, t'e vay I youst seen her charge beyonetts then back and come again.  Vell, I youst been heard peoples say somethings about mothers-in-law, but if she been Tracy's mother and Tracy been my wife, ten I got some mother-in-laws right from vere te git'em hand made.        .    .

C.  Don't speak so disrespectfully of Mrs. McGregor, Fritz, in my presence, whether she is Tracy's mother or not, she was my only and constant playmate in childhood, and further more she is my dear husband's first cousin.

F.  Dot vas true, 1 vonder how that come?

C.  Allie's mother was a Galbraith, Tom's father's sister. Allie's name is Alwilda Galbraith Branch. It is strange Tom's aunt should have married Col. Branch. The family were all opposed to it. But he went to the Mexican war and exerted himself as a soldier to reflect credit on himself and he succeeded in gaining quite a reputation for bravery and soldierly bearing and he being much better looking then than he is now, her father consented thinking he'd remain in the army after the war and thus necessarily be from home a great deal. But no sooner were the Mexicans conquered, than the young Colonel resigned and came home to Plantation life. Seeing he could do nothing but succumb to the inevitable, grandfather Galbraith deeded to her the View Mount plantation, which she owned until her death and which is now Allie's.

F.  And dot vas te fortune you spoke of dot vould been Tracy's ven she comed of age.

C.  I hav'nt said Allie was Tracy's mother. But in addition to the View Moub Plantation, at the death of the senior Galbraith, there was a legacy of several thousand dollars left to Allie, which is still untouched and drawing interest. My husband, and not Allie's father, is custodian of that.

F.  And then all dot raving about "my child, my child," dot crazy vomans put to her hearers, vas not all for noddings.

C.  Allie is not crazy, they say now. Since she found her husband her mind has been entirely restored, so I have understood. The last time I saw her she was convalescent but not entirely recovered.

F.  Didn't you told me Capt. McGregor and Miss Branch, were married in Richmond?

C.  No, I did not tell you Fritz, but I will tell you all about it, if you'll promise to keep the secret. It's something I never have told my husband. I think sometimes I ought to tell it, and then I don't know what might come of it and if Allie's reconciled without her child, I am sure Tracy's happy as can be.

F.  Nine, of dot crazy vomans been my mother-in-laws, don't you let it get away, you keeps him Dot vould been a secrets between you and me. Tell me about it Cleo, all about dot match team of runaways, I want to know all about Tracy's decendants anyway.

C.  Ancestor's you mean. Well, I'll tell you, and what comes of it concerns you, as Tracy's husband more than it will me.

F.  Vell, proceed, I youst itemize. (Takes pencil and paper from his pocket.)

C. Oh, that's not necessary, [Takes pencil and paper from him.] It's a short story; McGregor, and Allie got in love and as Colonel Branch, of course they knew would op, so it, they did not think of anything but a clandestine affair and under pretence of going to school in Baltimore, Allie, went there to live ostenciblyly with her aunt, the Colonel's sister. They married there or somewhere, but Aunt Elmira died. Capt. McGregor went on with the troapes was taken prisoner it seems and Allie, forsaken by everybody apparently, sought refuge in a Catholic Hospital, where Tracy was born and where she was when her father found her. Coming on home stopping to recuperate at Blue Mountain Home, they left the baby there, to all intents and purposes. But deluding Allie into believing the child dead, Col. Branch brought it to me to raise. You know the rest, he had just given it to me when you came up that time at the old hollow tree

F. Vat vas old Branch want to baby out of the vay.

C. Because it was, always intended Allie and my Tom should marry, and Allie's father, thinking it would be a hindrance, tried to squelch the whole thing. Allie was not supposed to have been married at all, and when after the war Capt. McGregor came through Baltimore hunting his wife, her relatives who have no intercourse with the Galbraiths, told him she was dead, and no one knew just how the thing was until Allie's father who could in no way get access to any of her money, being so reduced financially, and as Allie seemed hopelessly insane, and Tom had married me. and as from all appearance living next of act, in this case, cou'l do no harm, the old man bethought himself to reap some benefit from his daughter's alliance with the Union soldier, and sought thereby to replenish his impoverished exchequer, and proceeded to introduce measures to obtain a pension for his daughter. But lo and behold! When the regiment and company of the missing husband was given and evidence brought forward, Capt. McGregor was discovered to be still living—Captain no longer, but Major in the standing army, located in the West somewhere. The whole proceeding resulted in his coming on to claim his wife. But poor, poor man, his heart was most broken anew to find her so deranged. But I have understood that the sight of him recalled her to herself sufficiently to give the physicians some hopes of her ultimate complete restoration of mind. How complete this cure has been I do not know. She left here in company with her husband, and a special physician and I trust she is entirely herself again. I have never seen her since she went away. Her husband got leave of absence for six months and they traveled a good deal, but when they returned to the army by way of View Mount I was not here and did not see her. But we shall soon see her. Col. Branch expected them home last night, and if they come, as the house at View Mount and the furnishing are out of repair and as they will not want to replenish it for so short a time as they will stay, they will stay with us here. Tom has gone over this morning to conduct them here, and you shall see who is to be your mother-in-law.

F. But you don't let him got away.

C. But remember Fritz, before Allie's mind became disordered there was never a nicer, sweeter, more lovely creature than she was, and she is just such now, I hope if she is herself again. (Allie enters, apparently as crazy as ever, mumbling something inaudibly.)

F. (Pointing to her.) And I dinks she vas by golly.

C. Poor, poor thing.

F. Dot vas to been my mother-in-laws. Gleo dot vas a white headed lie you told me bout that vomans been made some sense.

C. Yes, but you promised it should make no difference with your affairs and Tracy, and you———

A. (Who has hesitatingly drawn near them)  Good—good people—I—I—oh—sweet lady—I—oh kind sir—have you—have you seen—have you seen a little—a little child to-day—a little bit of a baby girl—that looks like me?

F. Dot vas a funny gray haired baby vat looks like you.

A·  I'm—I'm its mother, I—I—[Laughs and cries and sings.]

> I kissed her to sleep last night, last night,
>     I kissed her to sleep last night,
> And laid her down in her trundle bed,
>     All curtained and soft and white,
> My vigils I kept but then I slept,
>     Alas! till the dewy dawn,
> And when I awoke and sought my child,
>     They'd stole her away—she was gone, she was gone,

Yes, they stole her away, and I'm—I'm so lonely. You haven't seen her—my baby girl? Here is a wee little dress, I took it off her myself just before I kissed—kissed her to sleep.  Oh, precious rag (kisses it) that wrapped my pretty, pretty child. Have you seen a lost child to-day that this would fit?

C. [Reaching for it.]  Let me see it Allie?

A.  [Snatching it back and holding it closely.]  Oh! no, no, no, do not take it away! 'tis all I have—except this, this little slipper, oh, angel feet that wore this dainty thing—that pressed this little sole, oh, precious pretty thing! [Kisses the slipper.] See it is worn some on the toe. [Laughs and cries insanely.] Oh, where! oh, where is my child, my child! [Walks across the stage.]

F. Dot vas to shveet, nice, lovely creature dot vas to been my mother-in-laws.

C. Hush Fritz, do be more humang that breaks my heart.

F. Vell, don't divulge, you promised not to tell. [Allie stands with her back half turnedto them, looking at them out of the corners of her eyes and listening intently.]

C. I did, I know. But I do feel dreadful Fritz, for the part I have played and am still playing in this affair.

F. You hear that now! Vell, if you told I am off to the regulars.

C. Yes, and right there is where Allie, with her husband, belongs.

F. Den I'd plow the mighty deep before I face a mother-in-laws like dot.

C. Well, I won't, I won't!

A. Sings:

Oh! where, oh, where is my sweet little babe,
    My sweet little babe so fair?
So chubby and round and dimpled her face,
    With her blue eyes and golden hair.

C. Oh! Fritz, Fritz, this is terrible!

F. But don't you let it get avay.

A. [Sings again :]

I scarce knew she was mine so little was she,
    She never knew I was her mother,
Until she was stolen away from me,
    Was stolen and given to another.

C. What harm could it be for me to let her know who and where her child is? [Allie listens intently unobserved by C. & F.]

F. Nine, you said you wouldn't let dot secrets git out from twixth you and me.

C. Well, God pity me!

A. (Aside.) *Ah! thank heaven I know who knows where my child is.* (Coming back.) Oh! sweet, sweet lady where is my child? Good, good sir, where is my child? Sweet lovely creature, oh, my precious, precious babe. You haven't seen her then, (cries,) oh, I'm so sorry, I thought you had seen her, good bye sweet lady, good bye kind sir. If you see a lost child who could wear this little dress and this dainty shoe, remember she's mine, my own, my own sweet babe, good bye, good bye.

F. Goot pye, goot pye. (aside) Goot pye, goot pye, of you said good bye vy don't you go? Of you vasn't going vat for you said good bye?

A. [Appealing to Cleo.] Good, good sweet lady where is my child? [C. drops into a chair and covers her face, with her hands and Allie moves slowly off the stage singing :

I kissed her to sleep last night, &c.

C. Fritz, this is terrible, unbearable.

F. But don't let it get away.

C. I feel I can never get forgiveness for what I have done, unless I tell her who and where her child is.

F. Dot vould break your vord and I am off to the ocean plue and Tracy vas in unmarried vidow before I'd face dot mother in-laws. Good bye I'm going out to te garden. [Goes out but hides where audience can see him.]

A. [Enters and sings and watches Cleo.]

My vigils I kept but then I slept,
Alas! till the dewy dawn.
And when I awoke I sought my child,
They'd stole her away, she was gone, she was gone.

C. Oh, this is terrible if she keeps on she'll drive me distracted, [sits with her face in her hands.]

A. Cleopatra Galbraith, look at me. [Cleo looks up and Allie snatches off the disheveled wig and torn outer garments and stands before Cleo a sane woman well dressed but gray headed, Cleo screams and hides her face again.] Behold your victim! Look at this gray head and say: "See what I have done." Look at this wrinkled face and exclaim : "This is where my fingers have touched." Search deeper and boast of my broken heart: "This, this is where I thust my poisoned daggar." Think of my wretched ruined life, and hiss through teeth that mighst well gnash mongst fiends in hell. "Ha! how well is my work done!"

C. [Half lifting her head and waving her off.] Oh! pity, pity while you blame, mercy! Do not curse me Allie!

A. [Stepping nearer and leaning over Cleo's bent form.] What had I done to be so foully dealt with by her whom I might reasonably have claimed as my most faithful friend? When in babyhood we nursed together from the same mammy's breast, did my infant finger nails inadvertently scratch fire from your black, black eyes that must needs reach out and sear and scorch my life, and wither

it to nothingness? Or yet when larger grown and in childhood we
sported through these spacious halls, or barefooted chased butter-
flies o'er the lawn at View Mount by what unlucky misshap did I
so fill your heart with vengeance? Or perhaps you loved the mooted
Yankee officer, and because you could not be his angel forsooth
you play the devil. Because he, ha, ha; he chose to love me, more
fondly. Or oh Cleo—Aha! Methinks you thought that were not
my beauty spoiled my reason left undisturbed, that I might
some day mistress be of stately Galbraith Hall.

    F.   (Behind the scenes.) Dot vas goin to pin my mutter-in-law.

    C.   Oh spare me Allie—Mercy—Mercy. You misjudge me so ;
you do not understand.

    A.   No, I do *not* understand.

    C.   I am not all to blame. You yet shall know all—*all*.

    A.   Enough of this. *Cleo where's my child?* (Cleo rushes to the
door and meets Tracy, a fifteen year old miss, in the doorway, and
turning they confront Allie.)

    C.   Mother there's your child ! child, there's your mother !

    A.   My child, my child !

    T.   Mammamamma! (They embrace and Cleo goes out.)

    F.   Dat vas a happy meetin. Dot vas goin to been myne vife
and mutter-in-laws.

    T.   Come sit down my mama dear. (They sit together on a sofa,
Allie fondly carresses Tracy by every look and action of affection.)

    A.   Oh my child, my long lost darling !

    T.   (Laughingly,) Yes my precious mama honey, I am so hap-
py to find you, I am happy anyway, I am always happy. Oh
dear, ha, ha, I wonder if this unbroken unalloyed happiness I feel
can always last, ha, ha. *Oh,* mama I am so happy.

    A.   Well, my darling I am overjoyed myself to know you see
so little trouble.

    T.   Trouble! so little trouble! Mama you are mistaken, I never
saw any trouble in my life, ha, ha. Except I thought you might
be living and of course I wanted to see you. But aside from that
I am sure my days have been days of peace and pleasure. But, ha,
ha, ha, just now I am particularly happy. Oh, dear I seem to be
living in some blissful dream.

    A   From which you may awake to grief some day, but no I
will not cause your young heart one little grief.

    T.   Oh, no you couldn't mama dear.

    A.   But pray my precious darling, if a mother might have her
daughter's confidence, what is the occasion of this ecstacy just at
this immediate period?

T.   Occasion? ha, ha, at this immediate period? ha, ha, ha.

A.   Why child you interest me a great deal.  Do tell me why you are just now so happy?  You can surely confide in me?

T.   Confide in you, ha, ha, oh, certainly, why shouldn't I?  Oh! dear yes, I'd confide in you, I'd tell you anything I would anybody else and more to but, oh, dear ha, ha, I—I—oh, I am so happy.  (Laughs.)

A.   Oh! my precious darling, what can so have captivated you.

T.   *What* can so have captivated me.  *Who* you mean, ha, ha, there now, oh dear, I've done it.

A.   Well, who can have so captivated you?  Who my dear?

T.   Oh; I don't know—I don't want to tell—I—I—who? oh, why mama dear, you of course, why shouldn't I be captivated with my own real mama when I have found her at last.  Why yes you mama I'm captivated with you.

A.   Do not try to deceive me my darling, you cannot.

T.   Deceive you, no honey mama no indeed.  You hurt my feelings, but I would tell you—what—who—

A.   Tell me darling, oh, you sweet, sweet dear what is it so interests you?

T.   Oh; dear mama honey I'm—I'm—ha, ha, [laughs and turns her face away,] I'm oh, dear honey mama, I'm.

A.   Yours are what my precious?

T.   I'm—I'm—*engaged!*  (Laughs and hides her face in her mother's lap.)

A.   Engaged! engaged for what?

T.   Engaged to marry, ha, ha.

A.   Oh; impossible.  You are a child, my precious child.  Impossible!

T.   No it isn't impossible, its true.

A.   Ah me, ah me, my child! my child, I have scarcely found you and now I must lose you.

T.   Oh, no honey mama you are to live with us.  Oh, dear I am so happy, ha, ha.

A.   My child, my child, God grant you may always remain so.

T.   Remain so?  Why yes, why shouldn't I?  I'll always remain so.

A.   Who are you engaged to, my darling?

T.   Oh, dear, he's the nicest fellow, oh, he's so funny—he's just the funniest fellow.

A.   Fellow, fellow, my dear is he a fellow, is that the way you speak of him?

T.   Fellow, why to be sure he's a fellow, yes, he's my fellow.

Speak of him that way? Why yes, to be sure, and he's oh, the funniest fellow.

A Who is he?

T. Who is he! Oh, dear he's so funny, he makes me laugh all the time, he says that is why I am so fat, I laugh so much. Ha, ha— he's so funny.

A. Who is he? I hope he's a very proper man, and of good family?

T. Well, he may be, but I don't care, he may be common. I am in Love with him, not his family, and he's good whether they are or not.

A. You don't comprehend me; I mean, I hope his is an old family.

T. Well, I guess it's old. They say he is anyway, much too old for me.

A. What kind of family is he of?

T. He came of the dutch family. But don't be too impatient Loney mama, you shall see him.

A. Be careful my child what you do. Do you know much of this funny man you are to marry?

T. Ha, ha, oh, yes, I have a speaking acquaintance with him, at least I think I know him when I see him. [A side.] I guess Fritz thinks I ought to know him.

A. Do not jest about such a serious matter my daughter. So often such dreadful mistakes occur where the contracting parties have only seen one another a time or two.

T. Well, I've seen my contracting party a half dozen times I think, and look here ha, ha, mama, I guess you thought you knew your business, and I know I do. Come lets walk in the conservatory. [They go off the stage and Cleo enters with Fritz made up as a German gentleman, Herr Geopper, who is followed by Flybarger, a dude.]

C. Oh, dear Herr Geopper, I am delighted to see you again. Welcome, welcome to my American home.

Herr G Tank you, tank you Misses Galbraith. Believe me I vas much bleased to see you and to see you looking so vell.

C. Oh, yes, I am quite well I thank you, I am rarely ever sick. And you say my father the Count is dead,

Herr G. Yes madam, I vas pretty much dead already by tish time. He vas been cremated good before I left Germany.

C. Cremated! oh, dear how shocking.

H. G. Nine, he vas youst pretty much dead before they burnt him. Here I brought you a leetle bit of his ashes, for a geep sake to shleep on for good luck.

C. Oh, no, oh, dear this is terrible.

II. G. I dole you vat you tinks vas more terrible as dot and ven I dole you I tinks you says he vould better as been cromated first and died afterwards.

C. Why, what is that?

H. G. Vot vas tish. He villed everthing to his son if he can be found.

C. Oh, yes, that is my brother, a year or so younger than I am. His name I believe is Frederick, yes. Well do they know anything of him. When I was in Germany, his where abouts was so much a mistery he was scarcely ever spoken of.

G. Dot vas true, but his fatter had a presentim ent dot he vas somewhere in America, and I vas sent oud here to see of I couldn't found him.

C. Well, how strange I am quite of my father's opinion, that if my brother can be found the estate and title should be his of course.

G. You tinks so? Vell, dot vas right, dot vas youst as well.

C. My poor father. I am right sorry to learn of his death. But still I cannot mourn as truely as I would if I had seen more of him. Let's see I think they said Brother Frederick, left Germany, when he was about fourteen or fifteen.

G. Yes, dot vas sixteen years ago 'bout.

C. Dear me he is quite a man by this time. How I should like to know him, and see what he is like.

G. I tinks we can found him. But, vat ladies vas tish? [Allie and Tracy enter. Flybarger, has all this time, been setting rubbing his silk hat with a bright colored silk handkercief.]

C. Oh, these are my dearest friends. Ladies this is Herr Geopper, Mrs. McGregor, and her daughter Tracy, Herr Geopper.

G. Ladies I vas most happy. [Allie bows coldly. But Tracy walks up and shakes his hand impulsively,]

T. Her Geopper, whose Geopper?

C. Oh, dear Tracy, how stupid of you Mr. Geopper, I mean.

G. Yes, dot vas right I vas most velcome to see you.

T. Well, yes I suppose so, quite welcome to make my acquaintance if mama has no objection. Indeed I think I shall be highly delighted with the acquaintance. In fact I am quite an admirer of Dutchmen.

G. Dutchmen, fraleen?

T· I see you are a dutchman of the regular old sort.

G. Dutchman, fraleen, Tracy you misstooken.

T. Oh, no I didn't, I know what you are. You're dutch as

:omes angry and strides up and down the room.)
:ome at all d·sconcerted at being called a dutch-
lat's nothing, I admire you for it. I just dote
id toe hair.
vite hair?
ouldn't I? Why, man I'm all broke up on a
ing to marry adutchman too. What's better?
me old fatty, I'm sure we'll get on well to-

ss ye don't been together, Madam [to Allie]
you she vasn't much like.
r, she is to much of a hoiden
this? (Stepping to Flybager.)
aghtless of me.
lings, dot vas no deeference. [Contemptuously.]
:y that is Mr. Flybarger, Miss McGregor, Mr.

what a namo ha, ha, what a funny name.
we weally.
t my servant.
ravelling companion. I am travelling with Herr

ed gentlemen. (As Flyborger, arose he sat his
as they sit Tracy sits down on his hat but
)
—my hat.
I sit down on your hat? Ha, ha! I thought I
lething. I'd better havo set on your head, I'd

ughter.
·ude.
:'s too bad. (Fly picks up the mashed hat and
:.)
ngs—dot vas no deeference. Mees Tracy could
ould mash his heart do—hey—Fly.
:hat's all right, you know. I beg of you don't
) That's all the hat I've got. It took my last
lived on one meal a day for two weeks to get
Now I must fast again.) Awe no, don't speak
assure you that was too utterly kind of you to
—awe, you know.
:oose you! Here let me have it, I can straight-
w. (Takes hat.)

Fly. Awe. thank you. Such awe, kindness is unparalled.

T. Nothing like it.

C. Herr Geopper, while Tracy repairs the hat please be kind enough to favor us with some selections of music.

G. Yes, mit pleasure.—I comply mit your request. (He sings.)

T. Here Fly, let's get from this, these old dullies are too stupid company for young bloods like you and me. Here take my arm.

Fly. Awe. You are too awfully gwacious—thank you.

T. Awe now, you can't be in awnest. By, by, Honey mamma. (Throws kisses.) Good by, Cleo, (to Geopper,) Me love's a rover, old lobster. Come on, Mr. Fly for short, lets take a turn on the lawn. You're too stucky for me, you need rumpling up. Say, by the way, did you ever horse-back ride any?

Fly. Well naw. You knaw Miss Twacy, I beg to protest. I—I——:

T. Oh no, no danger, nothing safer. I'll give you "old Hurricane," on his back you're same as in your mother's arms.

Fly. Awe! I suggest a game of croquet.

T. Ha, ha. Antediluvian Egyptian Mummy. Oh no, oh no.

Fly. Lawn Tennis, then!

T. Too tame, too tame. You must have a canter - a gallop. You'l look plum elegant splitting the wind, on "old Hurracane." Dear me, how he can scale creation. Old Hurricane went so fast with old Uncle Ned, he could scarcely sit his saddle, and he's a splendid horseman, and when old Hurricane did stop, Uncle Ned's breath was clean gone; he rode so fast. Oh he's lightning as well as Hurricane. Oh dear, he suits me, and you'll just be carried away with him.

Fly. I have no doubt—(with a forced laugh,) I'm afraid I——

T. Afraid now Fly, you ain't a coward, I know, and if you do get thrown, and I know you will; but the fun of it is to see how quick you can remount again. You can't any more than get your neck broken, and—well I guess you've got your life insured, its best. All judicious men like you, have.

Fly. Please dear, Miss Tracy, be so gwacious as to——

T. Excuse you. Oh no, sir. I tell you you'll think your name's Fly when old Hurricane cleaves the dusty air, with you swinging horizontally on to the bridle rein, two feet clear of his noble back. Oh, he's a hurricane right, and thunder and lightning too, and I guess you'll see fire and brimstone.

G. Goot py, Flybarger, if I never see you again vat message should I take to your only muther. (They go out, Flybarger quaking with fear.)

T.  Tell his sweetheart he *died* bravely.  Ha, ha.

G.  Vell ladies excuse me of I press my business, te sooner I find my man te biggerish my reward.  He, he.

C.  Herr Geopper, what are the particulars concerning my brother's absenting himself from home.  My indifference in the matter is excusable, as I have always been alienated from them.

G.  Vell, tere vas in Germany the land wehr, vat vas that part of the army dot keeps out invaders, and which every German boy has to serve three years, and ven young Frederick became the proper age for the army to join him, he youst made himself out of Germany quick.  He did not take to army life, and his father, te Count, always thought he came to America.  I have advertised extensively in te papers and in my absense from here some mail may come here, vich please preserve.  I been back——

C.  Why must you go so soon?  I had much to ask you concerning my father's affairs.

G.  Oxcuse me, fair ladies, I vill been back soon.  Of you be so kind I leaves Flybarger here until I return.  It he vas to been buried I pays te funeral expenses.  Goot by, Mrs. McGregor, goot by, Mrs. Galbraith.

Both.  Good by, Herr Geopper, we hope to see you soon.  (Exit Geopper, bowing low.)

C.  Now, Allie, friend of my childhood, friend of my youth let me explain.  As I told you, I am not at all to blame.  I have no hesitancy in saying that I should have had nothing to do with this painful matter, in fact, *known* nothing of it if it had'nt been for your father.

A.  My father!

C.  Yes, your father.  When he came to me with the child, he told me you thought it dead, and were becoming reconciled to the loss of it.  I was poor and friendless, and he offered to remunerate me for my pains, and after much deliberation I acquiesced.  But let me tell you Allie, it was, that the child being out of the way your chances for becoming mistress of Galbraith Hall might be rendered the more sure that I took the child, and, what is stranger still, it was also to establish myself as mistress of View Mount as your step-mother, if you please, that I finally consented to be an accomplice of his in defrauding you of your child.  This is the story, the confession I have to make, and I trust I may have your forgiveness.  The love I ever had for Mr. Branch left me however, the moment I knew he had always known I was entirely white, and only used my supposed African tincture as a pretext for not marrying me.

A.  My father!  Cleo do you tell me the truth?

C.  i do indeed.

A.  It is enough.  You are forgiven.

C.  Ha, ha, talk of angels &c.  (Enter Branch, old and feeble.)

Col.  Branch I have the honor to present to you Mrs. Major McGregor.  (Exit Cleo.)

Branch.  (Old, gray and feeble, leaning heavily on a cane.) How now, my daughter?  I meant to have seen you before you left View Mont this morning.  Army life seems to have addicted you to habits of early rising.  (Allie stands aloof and gives him little attention.)  Has the Major arrived yet?

A.  Don't speak to me.

B.  And why?

A.  It were enough to warrant repulsion to be a *fiend*, and doubly so that you have practiced your hellish deeds on me.

B.  How so Allie.  Indeed, I assure you, I understand you not.

A.  To fain dullness of apprehension, like any other coward were perhaps your most available method of hiding.

B.  What have I done? Allie. I assure you I have done nothing.

A.  Go ask my child, grown to womanhood in doubt and dread, as to who or what her parents were robbed of a mother's love and guidance, and (fiercely,) who you stole from me at the Blue Mountain Hotel, if what you have done is nothing.  Go ask my noble husband, whose very shoes you re unworthy to blacken, if to spend a life aimless and in desolation. that could only be made endurable, midst the trials of the distateful army life on the wild frontier, whose vicissitudes and battles were accepted, even welcomed gladly, as antidotes to a life of unspeakable misery, which per chance, happily they might put an end to.  Tricked by one with less than half his sense, fooled by one who is himself doubly fool, rudely sent adrift from an affectionate wife and sweet daughter, bereft of the consolation of the one and the animated society of the other, ask him, I say if what you have done is nothing. And I—and I, who am your daughter—I, who have spent months and years in a maniac's dungeon, *chained down* in a maniac's dungeon, the dampness of whose very walls dripping drops of poison, so unknown to warmth and sunlight, forbade that moss that feeds on damp rocks and darkness should dare to start there.  Chained down in a madman's cell, wherein God's sunlight never penetrated, a companion to varments that hunt a home in such a noisome place.  Toad and snakes—ha, (Screams.)  I see them now, slimy and green-eyed, feel them hop and crawl—ha! (screams.)  The very thought of which most drives me mad again.  And when made deft and cunning, me thinks, by the very imps that haunt the abodes of wild insanity I made my escape from such hideous habitation, I came away only to be ignored, shunned as an object repulsive and loathed by those who had known me, *loved* me, and called me sweet, sweet Allie Branch. (Shaking in his face her clenched fist she hisses fiercely,) Ask *me* if what you have done is nothing.

B. How did you learn all this objectionable conduct of mine.

A. Learn! bah! I read it in your cowardly countenance. *I say you stole my child, you dare not say I lie.*

B. And if I did, deluded girl, I only sought your good, your comfort an. you knew by hiding your accomplicity with that accursed Philip McGregor. The interruptory of my favorite plans. The inaugurator of all this trouble and disarrangement of my family affairs. But for him you had been comfortably established as Tom's wife and mistress of Galbraith Hall, and View Mount had been left to me, and Cleo apparently an octoroon, had been my mistress, ha, ha. But I could wish McGregor no worse fate than that he be custodian of my crazy daughter.

A. Have done with this! Retrospect if you will—pitiable old man. 'Tis little wonder with such a blackened past, and inauspicious future. Ha, ha, dote on what might have been 'tis all that's left you except that 'tis to die—Ha, ha; Go! View Mont: shall be yours to die in. I'll go to the army with my husband. Go, then to View Mont. and retrospection, cheap wine and Rostand Branch, ha, ha. And when old death, who stoops to kiss the vilest as well as the most noble, shall have blown his breath in your face, and you have left but breath with which to say it—gasp in the ear of your attendant this: Tell Allie, to come and close my eyes—ha, ha—Come I will and do it, and remembering that my mother loved you, I'll do it tenderly. (Laughing wildly she goes out.)

B. (Stands looking at her as she goes out.) Well my daughter I am sorry we are thus estranged, but if the physician who pronounced you sane is not himself somewhat demented I am. Ah me, by George it were enough to have been foiled in all my most sanguine hopes without thus peremptorily being brought to task for the guilty hand I played. That Allie knows me guilty it were folly to doubt as well as that she learned it all from Cleo. True, too true, it is that I have lived thus ignomineously. But to be told so is not. is not comfortable. Aye, 'tis worse, 'tis galling to my proud spirit that thus far has dared to my devilish deeds and none has ventured to gainsay or resist me, or question my motives. But it seems 'tis come to this—That I must now be roiled at. By George I remember my daughter's interview just now not pleasantly. And were I innocent I could heave a sigh, drop my chin on my breast, put my hand to my throbbing brow, and— and dote on my misfortuues and call myself abused, falsly accused and say with the cynic—I meet no congenia! spirits; the world understands me not. But being guilty—ha, ha! What can I do but laugh, (laughs.) And yet to be so insolently reproached in such approbvious terms by one I have petted a son, and chided— oh, by George 'tis only less miserable than to be scoffed at by myself. Not that I am thus become such a coward or perforce so valiant a knight of truth that I must with clasped hands and eyes turned heavenward exclaim: "My God my conscience hurts me!" No 't!s not that I have tried, how or wherefore that I repent me, but that I have failed, *failed*. Ah! *failed*. Years have come and gone since first my mother called me son, till I have known my three score years and ten. Yet have I not within my heart so many bits of gratitude, within my head so many bits of knowledge, or in my purse so many bits of "change." (Laughs.) By George! I must, as says my daughter, Mrs. McGregor, to View Mont and retro- spection, [laughs derisively] until I die. 'Tis with me ever to wish others dead even tried to kill them. Perhaps if on myself I tried my vicious thoughts and arts I'd prove me more successful. (Goes out.]

(Enters Flyberger, in a demoralized condition, hobbling on one foot, Tracy follows laughing.)

T. Hellow Fly, you are in sad plight. Who'd thought such a handy looking fellow could be so awkward. That is a beautiful gait you have, yeu went out on a gallop, but you seem to come in on a single foot.

Fly. Awe, Miss Tracy you know you have spoiled my beauty. Awe this is extweemly dissagweeable. Ouch—oh—excuse me Miss Tracy.

T. Ha, ha, what a wry face Fly let me arrange your twolight. [Toilet.] [She arranges his collar and necktie, etc.]

Fly. Awe Miss Tracy, you are too gwacious you know.

T. There you look better, I hope you feel better?

Fly. Yes, awe, bettah much bettah. [Attemps to step but limps terribly.] Aw, this is hawyble spwain in my wight lowah' ex- tweemity, its hawyble dissagreeable. Old Herricane is vewy hawyable to fall on.

T. Such a little man as you ha, ha. That wasn't what hurt your ankle. You effected your sprain by jumping up so quick while the horses weight was on your foot. You should have ex- ercised more paitence.

Fly. Yes, wealthy but I wenched it out before I thought.

T. Yes, there is nothing like presence of mind in a case of emergency.

Fly. Yes, aw, cewtenly. But my mind persuant or not prompted me to emawge from undaw, that lawge 'orse, ha, ha, Miss Tracy, that's pwetty good hey?

T. Oh, dear what sickly wit, ha, ha, but I'm sorry you're hurt. but I must go out to the garden where Fritz is. I just dote on Fritz say, he's my sweetheart, don't you tell anybody I told you, d'ye hear? Good bye, adieu—old Fly. Say, I'm sorry you're so mangled up, I'm afraid you can't row on the river with me this evening.

F. Aw, that would be delightful Miss Tracy, I assure you—a row on the wivah weath the moon's pale pensive light, aw, how extweemly wetweshing

T. Yes indeed we've been wanting to row across just above the falls its nearer and then we'd get a different view of the scenery.

F. Yes—aw—above the falls aw, Miss Tracy, is the watah there wewy wapid—aw—

T. Oh, yes, very indeed that's why Fritz and I never have rowed there before now, we're afraid we might be washed over the falls. That's why I wanted you to be able to row this evening, we'd watch you and if you went over safe we'd try it too. But if you went over the falls and got drowned we'd not try it.

F. Yes, aw—yes, certainly, I aw—The miscwies I suffah are still quite exqusheating aw, I think the injuries I sustained while widing will hawdly pomit of my enjoying the boat wide aw.

T. The injuries you sustained while riding, how ridiculous, you mean when you stopped riding, ha, ha. But I'm sorry you got hurt, [goes toward the door,] ta, ta—say, Fly, don't you want to chew my wax til I come back? Here. (Takes wax from her mouth.)

F. Aw, Miss Tracy believe me I appreciate your gwacious favah with evwy throb of my heart. (Lays his hand on his heart as he puts wax in his mouth, as Tracy goes out he exclaims as he strides with effected dignity toward her retreating figure with out streched arms.) Charming pusson! Angelic Queechaw! (A pain in his ankle causes him to relapse suddenly and uugracefully into a chair.) Oh, dear, oh, dear my foot. (He quiets himself and admires the boquet, and strikes asthetic attitudes before the flowers, when suddenly very loud crying is heard without and Fritz enters dressed as a large fat dutch girl—he cries boisterously.)

Fly. (Aside.) Oh, deah Lod, who have we heah, what trouble is this I wondah—I'll seek to know what grief so makes this pusson weep. I pray you pretty gull, why dost thou weep? (Fritz boo hoos, with renewed vigor.) Oh, peace, peace you wounded dove. What does so trouble you fond bweast? It bwakes my h:øt to heah you thus lament. Who has thus ruthlessly torn your tendah heart strings? Who? who could be so quel? Come untold to me your woes, you weeping willow and say who has hut yo' feelings so? .' ': '; Katrine. Who? who vas it dot made , pe cry. Who? Dot vas dot togoned dutchman. He youst most proke mine heart, boo–hoo. ·

Fly. Oh, cruel wretch why could he be so, *so* unkind.

K. I ton know how he could but he tid he youst said I vas'nt purty anyvay, boo–hoo–and dot he don't love me any more–boo–hoo.

Fly. Oh, sad, sad—it pains me hart.

K. He youst told me he vas youst foolin mit me anyvay and dot he don been agoin to marry mit me no dime, dot he vas youst a make me pelieve. Oh, dear mine pig fat heart vas youst proke up like cappage dot vas made up into crout. Oh, tear–oo boo hoo.

Fly. Oh, the pewfody of a man! But stay yo' weeping, sweet maid, I pray yon dwy those teaws, I'll—

K. Oh! oh! boo hoo–mine heart youst had an earthquvak, boo hoo.

F. Pway, pway, have done with weeping my pretty gaul, oh, bruised weed, oh, broken stock of golden rod lift up your bowed head.

K. Boo—hoo-o-o-o–.

F. I pwithee cease such weeping. (Aside.) It pains me heart so young, so fair, so tender, so delicately made with ah. Oh, me the would is quell. He was a hotless wetch that could so twiful with yo' tendaw feellings.

K. I feel youst tender as any vomans.

F. Yes, yes, I do pity you most hottily, you sweet potato dug too soon. Oh, pumpkin pulled before the frosts had turned you yellow. Delicious wataw mellon plugged *too, too* green. What can I do to comfort you?

K. Ouch! Ouch! Oh, tear, I feel so bate, boo—hoo—so bate.

F. It was a foul cwuel wetch that could thus twifle with yaw tendaw affections. But gwieve not loagaw I entreat you pwetty maid. If you want pwotection come lean on my strong arm.

K. [Aside.] It am don't been too strong enough.

F. If you sigh faw west come nestle yo' bonny head on my fond brest. [Imploringly as they step one step nearer each other.] Fly to my arms, to me and west thou tenderest of spring chickens. (Katrine inclines toward him.) Aw. me sweet submissive lamb. (Katrine lets loose all holts and falls against him, under her weight, which is too much for him he sinks onto a sofa behind him and Katrine lays on him almost completely covering him. (His thin legs and arms and head are all of him that is seen protruding from under her immence form, Fly, squirms a little and grunts.)

F. Ah! Aw—this—is—as—it—should—be. [Katrine sobs.] Aw—Mess Katrine—I—hope you—are—comfortable.

K. Yes, I vas youst been as comfortabler I vas could been I vas on sometings dot vas purty soft much.

F. I—I—think your gwief is all ovaw.

K. I tink your grief vas all under—[a long pause in which Katrine is convulsed wi h suppressed laughter and Fly, quiets and seems to try to settle himself to assume a comfortable position.)

K. [Aside.] I vonters of he don think I vas makin' a mashes. [She moves under which motion Fly, scrambles and tries to adjust her position so as to hurt him less.]

K. I youst hope Meester Flybuzzer, dot you'll soon get me fixed.

F. Yes, awe! there's no doubt but what you'll soon have me fixed.

K. Dot vas a purty much help ven you vas valking in a rough road to have some stout sticks on vich to lean. Vat a consolation to dot gentler sexes dot te can be shielded and sheltered by—by te boosome of one strong man. (Settling her entire weight on Fly.) Oh mine Got yat a refuge is here. Vat vas romans mit out a man in times of troubles! Te mans and te romans pelong close up togetter. (a long pause.)

Fly. I wonder to what length this is to be continued.

K. (Sings some German melody, and dozes—sleeps.)

Fly. [His, voice almost gone.] Oh ye Gawds! Ye Gawds! If—aw—there is only to be so much suffering in this weary world of ours, in as much as my pains awe so gwait I twust some po' fellaw beings may be so small, I pway. [K. snores loudly. Fly shivers and stretches out as if almost dead.]

Tracy. [Calling outside.] Katrina-a-a! You Katrina-a-a! [Just outside.] I wonder where that great gross specimen of Dutch womanhood can have gone to. Katrina! [She bursts into the room, Katrina, half awake and dazed, partly, sits up, but Fly remains motionless.] You impudent piece of impertinance. Get up from there this minute. [Boxes her.] You great lazy hulk. [K. squalls and Fly moves slightly and moans. Tracy jerks K up.] What are you doing here in the drawing room, you great

70

goose? [She discovers Fly. as K gets up.] *Mr. Flyburger, I am amazed!* [Fly. attempts to sit up, but falls back, unable to do so]. Katherine, what in the name of goodness are you doing, this far from the kitchen?

K. Of you blease, Mees Tracy, I vas just passin' to the well mit my pucket for vater, ven Mr. Flybuzzer shpied me from te wintow and called me to come here.

Fly. (Moans.) How am I put upon! 'Tis false, 'tis false.

K. You tid! you tid!

T. Mr. Flyberger, explain yourself, ha! ha! (Laughs.) A pretty spectacle. Katrine, leave the room. (Katrine dances out backward, singing.

K. Goot pye, Meester Buzzinfly. I meets you to-night in te moon lights vhere you say me do. [Kisses her hand to him and goes out.]

T. Ha! ha! It's "Meet me love in the Moon-light," I suppose? So Herr Geopper's traveling companion flirts with a Dutch servant girl.

Fly. Ye Gowds, and must I endure all this? My deah Miss Twacy, I assure you this ill-bred quechaw came here of her own accawd. I—I—

T. Oh, no differenc. Come on, I care nothing for yours' and Katrine's affairs. [Fly. attempts to rise. His knees and toes turned out as if he had been flattened out by the weight of Kathrine.]

T. Come on. [Pulls at Fly's. hand and observes how helpless he is.] Come on. Why, what's the matter with you? You don't seem to Fly.

F. Naw—I—aw—I seem to myself to be—aw—you knaw. I guess I'm pawallized.

T. Well, come, hurry, Fly, there is a gentleman waiting to see you in the library. He's a messenger from Herr Geopper Hurry, and then come back and lets hear what he has to say. I expect its something concerning this misplaced count.

Fly. Yes, awe, Miss Twacy, with the gwatest of pleasuaw, a messenger from Herr Geopper, awe.

T. Pray come, brace up Fly, you get along mighty bad. (They go out.)

[EntersMajor McGregor and Allie—Allie weeping silently.]

Mc. Come my darling, my precious darling, have done with weeping. You'll all but make me chide you for this gloominess.

A. I—I—yes, chidings were perhaps not undue.

Mc. I beg your pardon. I'd sooner chide my own heart whose

pulsings make me live—my own dear. But I pray you be not so sad. What right recent news have you of import so unkind as warrants all this gloominess, and causes all these tears? 'Tis not you think that I'm unkind?

A. No! no! I know you do not think so. (Sobs.)

Me. What can it be. I sometimes think I must mistake to think I've got my long lost Allie back. Where once were smiles and gay flippant talk, I now meet sobs and sad complainings.

A. My—my own Ph'lip, I sometimes doubt myself, so unlike am I to what I used to be.

Me. I see no reason now why this difference should be. I flattered myself—a hem—that 'twere enough to lend an occasional smile to your pretty face to have stumbled unto unworthy me once more. And I bethink me of times right often, when amidst the roughing of camp life in the West, your pensive smiles broke into light peals of rippling laughter, and made my heart so glad that I could e'en a most cry out my thanks to God that my angel Allie was restored to me, to rest upon my bosom so—(embraces her,) and cheer my lonely life.

A. (Sobs through smiles.) Yes, yes, I was sometimes then quite happy.

Me. Well, it strikes me strange indeed, that if you could then rejoice and laugh again over the meeting with poor, unworthy Phil, who had himself grown much unseemly cross and rough, that to find once more your precious child, so lythe and bright they say, would—would—ha, ha, (with a forced laugh,) make you laugh outright with excessive joy, would cheer the world with the gaiety of your spirits. Ah, my sweet pet, is it not so. I pray thee smile.

. (Moving away from him.) Oh hush. My Philip, hush. My dear, you almost make me vexed. Perhaps I may grow lighter of he rt, or at least not so despondent, but now—now—(cries.)

Me. There, there, come to my arms and cry it out upon my breast; you were so wont to lean on. [She complies, and he caresses her with every term of endearment.]

A. There, how silly of me to be such a child. I—I think I'm growing quite hypochondriac.

Me. I hope you feel better and will continue to—

A. Indeed, I'll try, if not for myself for you and my child, whom they have been pleased to call Theresa. Phlllip, it seems so sad, so bad indeed, that I must be denied the pleasure of naming my own child.

Mc.  Oh, my darling, you're almost selfish; I'm sure 'tis often done.  How given are mothers to bestowing the favor on some esteemed friend or kinsman of giving the baby a name.

A.  Yes, but ours was a circumstance quite different, the favor was not left me to bestow—not only the naming or saying who should name, but my child, as well, was stolen—torn from me and all thrust upon strangers.

Mc.  How wont you are to complain.  I'm sure, my dear, 'tis a beautiful name they gave her—Theresa—or Tracy as they've curtailed it.  Why, it suits her well, and quite easy 'tis to say.  And Allie, my dear, a hallowed name it is to me.

A.  And why?

Mc.  Because it was my mother's name.

A.  It was!  It was, my Phillip!

Mc.  Aye, indeed it was, and a sweeter name, the sound of which, could not be breathed upon my ear.

A.  Can this be true!

Mc.  True it is.  And even now, when to the past my mind reverts, and on my childhood days I muse, methinks, to my mother, I hear my father call, "Theresa, Theresa, I think—I think our Phillip needs a—needs a—" "Needs a what,' says she.  Says he, "I think our Phillip needs a—needs a --needs a thrashing."  Ha, ha, ha my dear, I pray you laugh.

A.  Oh! how glad I am to know this.

Mc.  Yes, indeed, and had angels wafted a name from Heaven, and whispered it low in its mother's ears, our child could not have had a name that suited me as well.

A.  And as I live but to please you, my own Phillip, I am glad our child is named Theresa.  But I must say it was really stupid of you not to have told me this before.

Mc.  Well, my dear, I could not tell you unless I was where you were, could I?  And when I am in your presence I can not even think of my mother, you are such an enchantress.  And now my own darling, I beg of you consider that all your troubles are as phantom like as this one of Tracy's name, and let your smiles make glad my heart once more.

A.  I'll try.  But what think you of this Fritz they say our Tracy's engaged to?

Mc.  Rather what I know—that is, that he is honest and good of heart; he's entertaining and not homely to look upon; and most of all he loves Tracy and Tracy loves him, and my consent was given them as soon as I knew she was mine to ask for.

Fritz.  (Who comes in in time to hear Allie's query.)  Mine

Got, I youst vish dot man vas been President some tay for sayin dot sometings, dot vas going to been my fatter-in-laws.

A. Yes, but is it not very objectionable that he is so *Dutch?*

F. (Aside.) Ditch! Ditch! Vell I guess I vas don't never been crazy as some ped pugs, and ticks and lunaticks.

Mc. No, that is nothing. As good people as live in this country are of German origin. And for his energy in her behalf in rescuing Miss Harriett Simmons, or rather the second Mrs. Branch, though the shock of that affair caused her death, she left him the bulk of the famous fifty thousand.

A. Ah well, remembering what trouble my father's interfering caused me, since Fritz is a good man I shall not object. (Fritz listens intently, and as Allie finishes the sentence rushes to her.)

F. I tank madam. I was your most obedient servant, I vas alway been good to Tracy, and vas alway been good to her still.

A. Take her Fritz, you have our consent. Let her will always be your pleasure.

Mc. And on both your heads rests a father's and mother's blessing. (They go out.)

F. Oh mine Got, vat vash home mitout a mutter-in-law.

T. (Calling outside.) Fritzie-e-e.

F. Hil de la hoo-he-e-e.

T. Fritzie-e-e.

F. Come to me-e-e.

T. (Entering.) Well, here I be-e-. (They run into each others arms and kiss.)

T. (Sings.)
Kiss me again honey,
O'er and o'er,
Your lips are so sweet honey,
Kiss me some more. [They kiss again.]

F. There, dot vas a regular breath taker.

T. Say Fritz, did you ask for me?

F. No.

T. Oh, you skeery goose!

F. Nine, they give you to me mithout asking.

T. And it's all settled?

F. Yah.

T. Oh dear, how delightful. (They do some song and dance business, until hearing footsteps they hastily retire, and Cleo comes hurriedly into the room much excited.)

C. Tracy! Tracy! Fritz! Fritz! Where are you?—here—quick. (Fritz and Tracy come slowly in from opposite directions.)

Where is Col. Branch? Was he not here but just this moment? Oh dear, how shocking!

F.  Mrs. Galbraith, vat's dot you say? Shocking, dot Col. Branch vas here in your house but just dish minute. Don't you know Col. Branch vas going to been my grandpa. Yhaw, yhaw. [Laughs.]

C.  You're not a grand-son that he'd boast of.

T  But really, aunt Cleo, what it—it—grand papa—ha, ha, how funny—what if Col. Branch was here? And tell me, do, why are you so excite d? The honorable gentleman in question *was* here but I saw him sometime ago mount his horse and gallop out of the lawn.

F.  Dot ain't nodings. He vas just always ride like some cyclone.

C.  How long since? There must be some mistake! *It cannot be!*

T.  No there isn't, auntie. What cannot be?

F.  Dere vas no mistookens about dot man going to been my grandpa. Hey, Tracy?

C.  List n here. This has just been received from View Mont. [Reads note.]

VIEW MONT, 11 A. M.

DEAR MRS. GALBRAITH:

Col. Branch—Master Rostand, but just this minute died. He came galloping up the avenue like a mad-man, bounded from the saddle, and scarcely had he time to get into the room and throw himself on to his couch, when hastening to him, he grasped me violently by the hand, and almost inaudibly—his voice being so nearly gone—hissed in my ear, "Tell Allie to come close my eyes!" And 'twas but said and he was dead. Your anxious servant, PAUL.

P. S. On examination his nether garments next his throat are saturated with blood, and I discovered a small, clean cut in the lower part of his neck, from which the blood still flows. In his vest pocket is a small pen knife, the blade of which is stained with blood. Come quickly. P.

Did you ever hear of the like? Can he have committed suicide? Oh dear, how dreadful!

F.  Dot vas too pad. Now I don't agoin' to had any some grandpas.

T.  It's dreadful, dreadful. But, then, Fritz think, we'll be some of the chief mourners. My! won't I look superb in crape?

C.  Why Tracy!

T  And besides, I'll look so demure and dignified.

F.  And I'll have some crape made on my hat for a hat pand, your like your tress dat it vas sometings a piece of, and I rite mit you, Tracy, and folks vil: said tere goes te two orphans. Thaw, yhaw.

C. Hush Fritz, for sha... Tracy, your conduct is shameful.

T. Ha, ha, what's the roe tor us to let on we're sorry here before you when you knos we are not. Just wait for the funeral, the anguish I shall fail. will be such as would make a listenes weep.

C. Think of your mamma, Col. Branch is your mama's father.

T. Thats all right. No. mamma can live at home in peace; that old Jimson weed's od town. Ha, ha.

F. If te lives at View Mont vould ve live at to cottage again?

T. No indeed, that's estirely too small an establish ent for the lady—Mrs. Fritz—I'm going to be. We'll live at View Mount and mama can live with us and at the army with papa.

F. Dot vas a purty geo. vay.

C. I do think you at are really heartless to think so little of this tragedy.

T. Aunt Cleo, we're not the ones to grieve—go tell mamma.

F. (Aside to Cleo.) You :t haf to be sorry as you for te Colonel. You remember hove you comes by Tracy, ha, ha. 'Dil my mutter and fatter tere to of (Mc. and Allie come in.)

C. (With a low bow.) Ah. Major I am delighted to see you.

Mc. 'Tis most pleases to ear you say so, I assure you. And that I see you is only easure to me than that I see you so well and looking so very ...

C. Oh thanks, most . Major. (In the meantime she has walked to Allie and pu' to a n around her) And my dear, how are you by this time? K er.) Indeed I trust that the sunlight of brighter days w. back to your sweet face the smiles it was once most wont to ...

A. Perhaps.

C. And I would my a were ever my privilege to bring to you such tidings that, t y caused you not to smile, 'twould be such as would make you art to throb with peaceful joy and sweetest satisfaction.

A. It can't always be though. I beg pardon that I thus anticipate what you are going to say.

C. Then you have heard?

A. I have heard noth g: but I apprehend your kind wishes, that you might always be a bearer of welcome tidings, were but a prelude to something y think my heart might ache at. I pray you then, my friend, proceed. The pursued beast of the jungle wild, may flinch and bo w at the piercing of his flesh by the first few shafts his assailants' hurl, but benumbed and paralized by the agony of a thousand stings he stands resigned and trembles not and scarce would move to evade a final thrust though 'twould deeper cut than any.

C. True,perhaps, but I am indeed a most unfortunate victim of cruel fate to have it made my duty to pour sad news into ears I fain would only whisper soft, in sweet tender words of cheer.

Mc. I know my wife as well as I appreciate the goodness of your heart, but——

A. What is this dire calamity.

C. Well, then, I have here news direct from View Mont, which says, your father—the Colonel is—not well—that is, he's dead.

Mc. So?

C. His dying message was to you, Allie, a weird but tender request. It was to come and close his eyes.

A. So soon.

Mc. So soon, my dear?

C. So soon? Dear me, was he not three score years and ten?

F. Nine. dot old man vas not dead mit infanticide.

A. True indeed, and if I did take from him his life I took but trash, when it was less than nothing, and sent him body and soul together. Not in the bloom of youth, to blast his life, scatter his mind to the four winds and 'eave him so to wander like some soulless thing, disconsolate, neither dead nor living.

F. Yhaw! Yhaw! Yhaw! (Laughs Fritz boisterously, who has been sitting apart with Tracy on his knee inaudibly playing William Matrimmaltoe. C. A. and Mc. talks apart.]

T. Let's play head acher, eye weaker and so on.

F. Vat vos dot.

T. Why head acher and eye winker and so on, don't you know?

F. Nine I don't know. I can vink my eye dot vay, (winks) but I don't got some headaches. I don't had enough vat puts pile in ter stomachs.

T. Well I'll show you how to play.

F. All right. You play headacher, and I play vink my eyes.

T. (Impatiently.) No, no, you don't understand.

F. How ten. I know vat you tries to foolish mit me. You. vant to git me vink me eye too you dot vay and ten you git mads and put a headache on me, nine?

T. Oh no. See here I'll show you. Hold right still [Touches with her finger, forehead, right eye, left eye, nose, mouth, chin, throat.] Headacher, eye winker, Ton tinker, nose stopper, mouth eater, chin jobber, gully, gully, gully. [Tickling him under the chin.]

F. [Laughs.] Vash dot it.

T. [Laughing.] Yes

F. Now let me do you dot vay. [They continue this playing awhile and go off the stage playing.

A. I was as happy once. [Pointing to Tracy.] Ah, Philip.

Me. Yes, my dear.

Fly. [entering.] Awe ladies and Major, [bowing], I ope I don't intwood.

C. Come in Mr. Flyburger.

Fly. If you all please and excuse me awe—I have some particular business, awe, in coming. Col Branch——

C. We know.

Fly. I beg your pawdon, awe, you know the sowoful pawt, but not the pleasant pawt.

C. What news have you; let's hear it, if 'tis pleasant.

Fly. Well, awe, not to tax your patience, awe, I will say—at once since Col. Branch's death it has come to light that he has, and has had all the time, the evidence to establish the fact, without a doubt, that this Mr. Fritz here, who is to marry Tracy, is none other than the missing Count, this lady's brother, for whom my Master Herr Geopper is in search.

A. How came you to know this?

Fly. Awe, excuse me yes, awe, I am the beawer of good news. I would not have you question me as to how I gained this information, or what were Col. Branch's object in retaining the desired information. But I beg you that you will have Mr. Fritz called immediately, that I may question him further, and ascertain the information that I want, and hasten home, awe, to get the reward. [Enters Tom and Uncle Paul, quite feeble. Salutations exchange.]

Tom G. Uncle Paul has something he wishes to say to this company.

A. Uncle Paul proceed, I am impatient.

C. Yes, Uncle Paul, we'll hear you with great pleasure.

P. Well, I hope then, that in saying what I do, you will none of you think I say it with the least disrespect for my late masters. For though he had his shortcomings, the comings of all on us are none too long. I tell it for two reasons. Firstly. My Master said I should tell it, and secondly, it will do no harm to tell it. Well, the Colonel has always known that Fritz was the only son of a wealthy German Count, and I knew it too. As, also, we both knew Miss Cleo was his daughter  In keeping this all a secret, had he have married Cleo, which he would have done, could he have made known that she was white without implicating himself in the purloining of the child—he hoped to have the estate of her father settled on her when the Count, her father, died. But being missed of this, the son being usually made the heir, his next attention was given to Fritz, who he learned in a correspondence he had with a friend of his, the U. S Consul of Bavaria was the son and heir. He intended once to try to establish the impression that Tracy was the fruit of a secret marriage between Fritz and Allie ; keep Allie c nfined in a mad house, and put Fritz where he'd not be so inconvenient. But this plan became impracticable if not impossible. His last scheme was to have Tracy marry Fritz, and send Fritz, as he said, to Dutch heaven ; have himself made Tracy's guardian, and, as he also said, go down to a ripe old age, in a fine coach-and-four. But it seems he gave it all up, for it is evident he committed suicide.

A.  Will night ne'er grow so dark it cannot darker grow !  Ah, my mother, was there no fiend mongst hell's infernal throng that thou mightest mated with and found a spirit less in conflict with thy sweet angel nature !  [To P.]  Is there more of this old man, of him who had short comings?  [Laughs wildly.]

C.  Left he no written evidences, no papers, no documents of any kind—no Bible, perhaps, with births recorded, will clearly show, and quick, that Fritz indeed is my brother—my own brother?

P.  He did, Miss Cleo—this packet, (presents it) containing all that he had in black and white relative to the case in question—the letters from the Foreign Consul together with a copy of Fritz's birth as Count Frederick's son ; also a minature degnereotype taken with old Koehler the Count's old reliable servant, he said I should put into your hands.

Fly.  Awe, what bettaw evidence could one desiaw ?  [At this juncture Tracy bursts into the conservatory laughing gaily, and followed closely by Fritz with a watering pot of water in his hand. As he enters the room he handles the pot so that the sprinkler sprays water on the guests, who try by dodging to escape the wetting, Flyburger especially.]

C.  Oh, Fritz! Fritz !  Uncle Paul has such delightful news to tell you !

F.  Vat's dot?

C.  He has undisputable evidence that you are my own brother.

F.  Vell, vat of dot, done I been always saying sister dis and sister dot ?

C. Yes, but you are my *sure enough brother!*

F. Yhaw; vas dot so?

P. It is, indeed. sir. (Exit Paul.)

F. Yaw, yaw, Gleo; vile ve vas mit Tracy lives in to cottage make believe sisters and brotters—done ve been tries hardt to make peebel tink a lie dot vas te truth. Gleo, youst let me skveeze you mit a brother's skveeze. [Embraces her. As he sits the pot down, as it by accident. he pours water down Fly's back, he stooped over talking inaudibly to Tracy. Fly jumps up and makes becoming ado about it.]

Fly. (With an attempt to seem not out of humor.) Dear Mistaw Fwits, awe, that was a cold weception, awe, ha, ha.

F. I youst tinks you receives a cold from dot.

Fly. (Bowing low.) I, awe, beg pawdon, ladies, gentlemen, awe I have to make my bow, to say to you, awe, I can't wemain with you longer. (Puts his hat on, in which Frits had poured a little water, throwing the same over his face as he places it on his head.) Awe, this is vewy disagweeable. Fawwell, awe. [pointing to Frits] Behold the missing—the long sought' for Count. Adieu, aw revawr, (with attempted dignity) I go to my weward.

F. Vat vas manesuns laid up in heaven. (Fires a pistol at Fly who tumbles out of the room.)

G. Well, Frits, in behalf of your friends, and—with pleasure. —relatives, I congratulate you on your good fortune. You are immensely wealthy, and your title of Count came not single-handed

T. Oh, Frits, Frits are you a real live Count? Oh, dear, I'm so glad I got in love with you—I thought you was something besides just a dutchman.

F. Yah, yah, I vas purty glad of te moneys. and, [to Me and A] Major and Mrs. McGregor, I vas glat you said I should get your child vile you tought I was youst poor Frits. But after all. wealth vas youst an umprella dat vould keep out te rain, but it vould keep out te sunshine do; and vile it vas purty convenient sometimes ven tings vas purty much cloudy, it vas youst as unhandy and in de vay ven you don't needs him; and you vas always afraid somebodies vas tryin' to shteel him, and he vas sure to pe sbtole, and ven he vas stole, your monies and your umbrella vas just like anypody else's. You done been able to identify tem and proves him in court. But I vas glad you know I vas of an old familias and goot. I game to this country to evade being pressed into te landvehr, in which every German boy has to serve three years.

T. And now you are a sure enough, big, live meat Count?

88

F. Yes, i vas a Gount, and you vas a whole county, init a court
houses and jails; and I vas goin to hold court in your court house
every days, ound you can lock my heart up in your jail and lose te
keys forever.

T. Oh, that's just heart bursting ecstacy! But say, Fritz, the
woman isn't a county, she's a Countess.

F. Yah; you vas goin to been two counties—dree counties—
whole shtate of counties—and some day, listen, ven ve got some
leetle poys, I been te old governor.

T. And you'll be a Count with a big mustache, and I'll be a
Countess—so grand and tremendous—the very earth shall resound
with my majestic tread. Won't I look just too killing? [Struts up
the stage.]

F. Me, too! Me, too! [Starts after her. They promenade a
circle and come back to center of the stage.]

T. Yes; but say, Fritz, that's in Germany.

F. Yaw.

T. They don't have Counts and Countesses in this country.

F. Vell, in Germany we been Count Frederick and Countess
Theresa.

T. But here?

F.

Here in tish country, te land of te free.
And te purtiest, shveet girl dot ever I see,
(Puts his arm around Tracy.)
Where all mans vas sovereign, if he vas Pres'dent some tay—
Te land of brave boys, of te Blue and te Gray,—

We vas simply Tracy and Fritz in America.

(CURTAIN.)


DISPOSITION OF CHARACTERS.

Mc. and Allie,          Fritz and Tracy,          Tom and Cleo.

www.ingramcontent.com/pod-product-compliance
Lightning Source LLC
Chambersburg PA
CBHW032352020726
47499CB00008B/2718